CHARACTERS

The chain binding Engulf's body shattered. Unexpectedly two wings popped open, one white, the other black. With a bright light radiating from his soul, he entered the roasted body that was on the dwindling pile of wood.

Detective Mullson, with what appeared to be blood trickling from his eyes, extended his hand toward Father Andrew.

"By the way, my name is Trevor Mullson," he said. They shook hands. "Never got the chance to formally introduce myself," Mullson continued.

"You're the one," a shivering Father Andrew uttered, before falling into a trance.

The dog rushed to the back of the plane, echoed a bark, dived over a trolley and entered the galley. After sensing something in the darkness, with killer instincts he preyed upon the unknown. His ninety pounds of raw muscle was no match for whatever was inside that room...

"Somebody's got to do your job," Jack blurted, to Agent Hill. "Better watch your wife."

"Jack?" said Agent McKoy, in disapproval.

Book by R.J. Green

TANNY ANDERSON
Barefoot, Prickles & Thorns

SEARCHING

FOR THE ENEMIES

R.J. GREEN

ZYFEX BOOKS
http://www.rjgreen.net

ZFX BOOKS

This book is a work of fiction. Names, organizations, places, events, and incidents either are the product of the author's imagination or are used fictitiously.

This title is available at special quantity discounts for bulk purchases for sales promotion, premiums, fund-raising, educational, or institutional purpose.

ISBN-13: 978-0615488912
ISBN-10: 0615488919

ZYFEX™ BOOKS
www.zyfex.com

PRINTED IN THE UNITED STATES OF AMERICA

"People remembered you by the bad you did, if you gonna do bad, give them your best."

WAR

War is the heart of men who failed par…

The control of population within its evil bars…

Lies and betrayal that reflects beyond the stars,

the torturing or time that burn within its jar…

The amputating of limps, the sizing of scars…

War is measured by the size of your car,

and the gasoline that power it on the road paved with tar…

It's the extra land space you've been asking for,

the life of others that lied in bloody reservoir

War can only be defeated by peace,

and it is in every man's reach.

Acknowledgments

I would like to thank everyone who worked on this book, my insightful editor, Joan M. Roberts, and the wonderful people at Zyfex Books. To my family and friends who encouraged me not to give up on my dreams. Thanks to my current and future fans.

Author's Note

For the purposes of this story, I've bent some of the rules of police and military procedure and also created my own fictitious Gods and tribe.

CHAPTER 1

A lready, it had been a few months into the year twenty-twenty. From the depth of the Congo, in the thickest of woods, giant trees towered above to form a dense canopy. Secrets lingered on the surface below, at an area barely penetrated by the moon glistening through the branches of a barren tree that had been cursed by God himself for over a thousand years. This tree acted as the marker for a grave, a mound of dirt surrounded by stones, untouched by plants, erosion or any other natural elements. The outside world feared the curse, the grave was forgotten, and no lives prosper within the vicinity.

A creature of the dark scurrying over dried leaves broke the silence of forever quietness, with eyes beaming like an owl it emerged from behind a pile of stones and sniffed toward the grave. A RAT! Not your typical house rat; about twice the size of an American football and whiskers half the length of her body.

BOOM! A huge fist thundered its way to the earth's surface and grabbed the rat before it even got a chance to react. The fist clenched tighter and tighter, until the rat was squeezed out of its skin. A sudden chill hovered above.

The silence was yet again broken, this time by the purring of cats reverberating in the distance, getting louder as if approaching. Hidden by the cover of darkness, death emerged from the grave and scouted the woods. The creature, wobbling along like a human, stood more than six feet in height. With the instinct of a hound it traced a faded trail of blood scattered by the wind. Finally, in the distance glows of flames flickered. The creature advanced toward the light, slowly. After a thousand years of resting it didn't care about picking up the pace.

Just ahead a group of people gathered around an unlit pile of wood ready for a bonfire; their faces were colored red and white with matching costumes covering only their pubic areas. Most of the tribesmen clenched onto spears while others held torches; they jumped and moved in a well coordinated and circular pattern shouting words of an ancient language.

The chief lifted the prize above his head, still alive it squirmed as blood gushed into his palms, trickling down the back of his hands all the way to his underarms. Hanging around his neck, he wore a chain made of ivory that had a knife hanging like a pendant, dripping blood.

"Mumba tumba alanga!" he bellowed, giving thanks to the food.

The crowd wailed as their leader sunk his teeth into the heart and chewed away at the flesh, squeezing and sipping as the warm blood squirted out, before passing it on from the highest to the lowest of ranks. Every man and woman took a bite and licked whatever blood remained, until it was all gone. They used a torch and fired up the pile of wood.

Not long after, the aroma of their feast wandered in an unusual wind ruffling the top of trees. The people, mesmerized by the smell of their treat, didn't sense the danger lurking in the dark, even when the sounds of crunchy dried leaves and twigs snapped in nearby bushes and painful growls came from an area filled with thorns and razor sharp rocks.

Stretched and peeped, they kept blocking whatever was on the fire giving of such wild meaty stench mixed with the charring of rubbers and cottons. The link was finally broken to allow a moment to toss a quick glance. From all the heart pounding, sweating, eye popping —

WHAT THE HELL!

Jaw dropping. Wait a minute.

The face concealed with twigs and dry leaves had begun to blaze, the body, wrapped in an Armani black striped wool two-button suit with single pleat trousers, melted away. A business outfit of such caliber had no place here in the middle of the jungle.

For centuries only the 'Canni-tribe' had being roaming these forests. They worshiped the sun, feared the full moon, and feasted on strange looking two-legged animals after their ancestors ate the primates to extinction. They held a treasure scores of men hunted, but never returned— the legendary knife of Satan, which the Canni had no knowledge of. To them it was a gift that fell from the sky many, many full moons ago, piercing the heart of the then reigning chief, they claimed he was chosen by the Fire God. His generation ruled ever since and as a tribute to his bravery, the current chief used the knife and plucked out the heart of the tribe's sacred food.

The chest area was dampened with blood; a man was resting on that pile of wood, got to be. It was difficult to tell if the fellow's complexion was dark, or a well done roast ready to be eaten in some parts. A white crow braced for landing and perched on a nearby limb. It squawked loudly as the flames intensified. Sparks crackled. The body sizzled. The people drooled.

Still hidden among the shadows, the man like figure came to a standstill just a few feet away from the rowdy bunch; at the speed of light the creature darted into the heavens, as a black dove perched on a branch opposite the white crow.

A few minutes later the mysterious figure came crashing from the sky, hurling rocks and dirt upon hitting the ground, the place shook as the thing landed on its two feet, close to the body on the blazing fire. The native people were transfixed by the enormous power the stranger displayed. Not long after a thought came to the chief, he gripped the knife hanging like a pendant, the people knew what they had to do, and came swiftly towards the man-like figure.

Tall and muscular, covered in mud, and bound by heavy-duty chain wrapped around the body, the creature stared at the tribal people drifting towards him. This man is Engulf, as old as time itself, yet vibrant and youthful. He seeks one thing— the crown of his father. He spotted a particular knife the leader of men had been wielding. Already he could taste the victory as the world crumbled beneath his feet, the heaven was within reach, but first he planned to fulfill his mission. He glanced down at the dead body and knew the time was right, if only he managed to get a grip of himself and forgive Jason for what he'd done a thousand years ago.

Engulf recalled those images vividly, as if yesterday: the scent of the crisped air, the sun kissing the backdrop of a mountain peak reaching into the heavens, as it descended. Pines, firs, junipers, larches, spruces, and yews cluttered the higher region. At the lower section bordered by a lake, colorful flowers and shrubs scattered. On a patch of land, in the middle of the lake, towered six trees surrounded by flowers and rocks. Birds sung, rabbits and hares hopped along, lions roared to boast their dominance, but on this mountain the children of the Gods played. Good versus evil, God versus Satan. Engulf versus Jason.

A youthful Engulf stood on the mountain, his white robe blew about in a rush of evening breeze, from his shoulder a pair of wings extended more than a fifteen foot span, perfect teeth, face symmetrically aligned with powerful jaws, and a body that inspired every woman's fantasies. He was grasping a mighty sword in one hand, his eyes penetrated his prey — a black angel around early thirties, also dressed in white with a huge pair of black wings jutting from his shoulders. This man had a muscular physique that gave him a sensed of invincibility.

In a silver flash Engulf swung the sword towards the head of the other angel.

Jason stood tall and didn't even blink.

"I have always helped your kind," he said, with a smirk across his face.

Engulf turned and walked away, a few feet later he came to a standstill. "Yes, that's good," he said, "but you also betrayed my kind."

Jason was startled for a moment. Laughing out of control he finally regained his composure. "When're you going to give up, Engulf?"

"The quicker you die the merrier."

"What about the prophecy?"

"If I behead the first Son of God?"

"You better believe it," Jason whispered. "It will happen, even in death."

"You lost your head," Engulf teased.

Jason, shouting at the top of his lungs, sprinted toward Engulf. It was then Jason's head was totally separated from his body. The day became night, the wind turned into fire and ravaged the land, consuming Engulf who'd being resisting with all his might.

The chain binding Engulf's body shattered. Unexpectedly two wings popped open, one white, the other black. With a bright light radiating from his soul, he entered the roasted body that was on the dwindling pile of wood.

The tribal people scrambled away in fear, after they looked death in the eyes and acknowledged his creation. The power the stranger wheeled was of an angry God, and his curse was beyond their control. They hid in nearby bushes and waited for their leader to make the next move.

"The time has come,' Engulf bellowed. "RISE children of God!"

The crow and dove became lifeless and fell from their branches, hitting the forest floor with a thud, they smashed into pieces.

The Dead body crawled out of the fire in agony. Engulf pointed at the badly burnt resurrected body. "And you shall be called Wrath."

Wrath faced Engulf.

"What have you done?" he asked, with a New York accent. He sniffed the air and tried to figure where the strange odor was coming from. "What the 'uck is that," he said beneath his breath, "smells like roast dog."

"Open up your heart to me Wrath," said Engulf.

"My heart?"

"That's a small price to pay for your life."

"My name is not Wrath!"

"God cast me here on earth. I'm just doing my part."

Wrath used both hands and grabbed the back of his own head, "Why me?"

Tribal people approached slowly; more joined with each step forward. They crept up with spears ready to toss, arrows pulled back, bows pointed at Engulf and Wrath. With all the weapons they had there was no comfort as to what they were confronting. The bravest of men were shrunk to cowardice, but God himself understood this creature was beyond humankind's control. No cannibal processes the enzyme to digest the cursed flesh of Engulf. The maggots and vultures had timeless opportunity, but all refused.

Something about the tribal people gave Wrath the creeps, in the shadow of his past he remained, only if he knew what they'd done to him. Engulf would be more than happy to reveal all those dirty secrets, but first he must conquer Wrath, for he needed his help to carry out an ambitious plan he'd been cooking up.

"I hate rednecks!" Wrath confessed. He stood looking at the red paint dabbed around the neck of the Canni people.

A tribesman emerged from behind a tree, closer to Engulf who had been facing away. With all his might the man threw a spear toward the beast.

Engulf turned around just as the spear neared the back of his head. In midair the spear suddenly stopped about an inch away from his eyes. Engulf was furious, his anger building, causing the spear explode into small particles.

Wrath spotted the man who threw the spear, his body stood with blood gushing from the neck, after his head got ripped off by an object moving faster than his eyes could see. Wrath looked around and had no clue when and where Engulf had disappeared to. As his confused mind roamed, a hand covered in blood tapped his shoulder. He leaped back in fright, and stared at Engulf who held his victim's head.

Engulf's wings disappeared into his back, making him appear more human. He tossed the head toward the Canni people who were becoming more aggressive.

"Mal alanga!" the chief screamed "bad food," pointing towards Wrath and Engulf.

The people, shouting at the top of their lungs, ran toward Wrath and Engulf. They came to a standstill when they heard the sounds of a cat purring echoing from the midst of the forest. The purring got louder and louder.

The Canni people bundled on each other in fear. Like hyenas scavenging carcasses, domestic cats emerged from the dark, and devoured the flesh of the tribal people, leaving only bloody skeletal remains in their path. Wrath hid behind Engulf the whole time. Engulf had the power to help, but in such a desperate time he seized every ounce of opportunity.

"You made the right choice," he told Wrath.

"What choice?" Wrath asked.

"By my side you'll no longer fall victim to the condemnation and degradation of what it is to be your kind," said Engulf, extending his hand towards Wrath.

"I'll never be a part of you," said Wrath, refusing to shake his hand. "Even if it means eating my own soul!"

The swarm of cats came toward Wrath and Engulf. "Man is a dignified animal," said Engulf, eying Wrath up and down. "Yet arrogant in the grave. Go ahead. How can you eat what's not yours?"

Wrath walked away without saying a word.

Engulf squeezed his fists and bit down on his teeth, a wretched expression flashed across his face. "We will be waiting!" he added, before vanishing into thin air. He gave off an evil chuckle in the backdrop. "You have more power than expected."

Wrath wandered the forest seeking a way out, his body morphed with every step, as the grip of the dark world rushed through his veins, unleashing powers beyond his control. Destiny had a calling, but why now? In his before life he came to this place, this country, this jungle — to acquire Satan's dagger. Now he got more than what he'd bargained for.

"What's happening to me?"

The forest shuffled to seek shelter from the inevitable — an unusual thunderstorm threatened the break of day. A bolt of lightning shattered a towering oak, ricocheting, before striking where the remains of the crow and dove scattered. Like opposite poles of a magnet thcir body parts began to pull together, flesh reattached, feathers sloppily rearranged and out of place by standards of nature. Out of death comes life, and life in all forms are precious. If only one wasn't blinded by judgement, the beauty of creation would reach the hearts of the wicked.

Nevertheless, a black crow and a white dove expanded their wings and thrust their bodies at the mercy of the wind. Each came as a messenger of their Gods, and away they returned with a piece of the other, in the opposite directions. Wrath looked towards the sky and extended his hands.

"Nooooooo!" he bellowed, in a high-pitched voice, piercing the universe.

CHAPTER 2

An old-fashioned three story house, outlined by a full moon hovering above, stands on an acre of land on the outskirts of a small New York town. Coniferous trees stand cluttered at the back further away from the house. About fifty yards from the main road, foot prints in the snow lead to the front door, getting deeper as they neared the house. The howling wind tossed snow against a window where a light flickered from the depth of the house. A deer scurried away as a gutter squeaked loose, hitting the ground, rocketing snow in all directions.

Inside the living room, by the fireplace, Father Johnson sat on an antique rocker. About seventy and wearing a priest outfit he used a fork to ruffle the wood, giving the place a warm glow. The whole room was jammed with antique furniture, figurines of the Virgin Mary, crosses of the messiah, and other religious sacraments. A small television, resting on a stand at one corner of the room, was on, but fuzzy.

"Revelations twelve verse seven," Father Johnson recited. "And there was war in heaven. Satan was cast to the bottomless pit for a thousand years."

He listened to a shrilling sound that made goose bumps rise at the back of his neck — the one Wrath thundered from the other side of the globe.

The television showed people panicking after hearing the weird sound, natural disasters ravaging different parts of the continents, priests from various religions praying, and the faithful getting ready to depart this miserable life as promised.

"But after these things he must be released for a little while," he continued. "But worse is to come. His son Engulf…" Father Johnson had been preparing for this moment for more than forty years. Whatever was happening in the forest of the Congo he felt somewhat responsible. But in the meantime he must wait. "Corinthians 5 verses 10. For we must all appear before the judgment seat of Christ; that each one may receive the things done in the body."

Three months had passed and the world didn't come to an end, as predicted. Most people had forgotten about the whole thing and were back to their normal lives after swearing they would kick the bad habits if they made it through what appeared to be Judgment Day. From all corners of the globe governments became more suspicious of each other, yet there was no scientific explanation to what may have caused the shriek.

On earth, people were making wishes to shooting stars that had been falling more than typical, especially the past few nights. Little did they know angels had being arriving by the thousands, hidden among men they prepared for the final battle, if the chosen one failed.

A Jumbo jet rocketed across the sky, leaving an undaunted trail as it left Central Africa and headed for Europe. Inside the jet something peculiar was happening. Not that anyone other than Trevor "Detective" Mullson noticed. He had been seeing the dead, but he just didn't know, as of yet.

In first class he sat at the right side of the plane. He was a well built fellow, about mid-forties, sporting a fine designer suit. He had Brown eyes, dark hair with a slight trace of grey. He ripped off his jacket and flung it across his lap, tugged on his tie, checked his watch several times. Sigh. Mullson sneaked a glance at a white fellow wearing a priest outfit that sat next to him.

The man in the priest outfit is Father Andrew, mid-sixties, clean shaven. His hands rattled as he read a section from an old textbook resting in his lap. His voice lingered in his head, "When the soul becomes separate, and the mind gets crisscrossed…" He squinted at Detective Mullson and could have sworn he saw an image of a skeleton. Father Andrew wanted to make sure he was not hallucinating. For in his living days he'd seen it all. Sweat splattered over his forehead. Rubbing his eyes while shaking the thoughts from his head, he spotted a black gentleman.

"Are you okay Father?" said Detective Mullson, with a light Jamaican accent.

"Yes, and you," Father Andrew replied, with an English accent.

"I guess I am," Mullson sounding a bit more confident.

"This is just the beginning, Mr. Mullson," Father Andrew whispered.

Astonishment gleamed across Mullson's face. He was quite sure he hadn't told anyone his name, especially when on mission to Africa. In his line of duty he'd learned to trust not a soul.

"Have we met before?" he asked.

"Just keep yer guards up," Father Andrew warned.

"Is this a curse of some sort?" said Detective Mullson, with a broad smile.

At the back of the plane a deranged man got up from his seat and began to run about screaming.

"I'm not crazy!" he said. "Do I look crazy?"

A drop dead gorgeous flight attendant, Asian, about mid-twenties, hurried towards the ranting man. Her name-tag read: NINA.

"Sir, please calm, everything's gonna be alright."

In first class, Mullson braced against his seat and reclined it to help release the discomfort along his spine.

"You look rather familiar," he said to Father Andrew, after his detective senses tickled. "Could have sworn I spotted you in Bangui."

Father Andrew eyes widened, a grin finally shot across his pale face.

"You're the only one who noticed," he whispered.

A white couple in their mid-sixties sat directly across from Mullson. Mrs. Jeft, a short rosy cheeked lady, loved a good gossip. Mr. Jeft, who towered over six feet and five inches, warned her about being nosy, for she always gets stressed over other folks business, but that didn't stop her from eavesdropping on Mullson's conversation. She slid on her glasses then peeped towards Mullson, an unpleasant look overshadowed her rosy cheeks. She took off her glasses, cleaned the lens in her coat, and slid them on for the fifth time. Still she couldn't figure who Mullson was talking to. She blamed the decades for her withering sight, now her mind was racing more than ever, her head pounded.

Detective Mullson, with what appeared to be blood trickling from his eyes, extended his hand toward Father Andrew.

"By the way, my name is Trevor Mullson," he said. They shook hands. "Never got the chance to formally introduce myself," Mullson continued.

"You're the one," a shivering Father Andrew uttered, before falling into a trance.

Forty years earlier, outside of a hospital in Montego Bay, Jamaica, after emerging from behind a cloud, the moon was glowing like a red hot charcoal. Two stars hovering above the hospital were painful for the naked eyes to view. The sounds of insects, now flattened by the minute, was somewhat unusual for this part of the country. Only the whispering of cats painted the backdrop, almost as if night stood still as something lurked in the darkness. The ferocious mongrels habitually scavenging the parking lot were nowhere to be found.

Five men in the shadows, wearing matching ankle-length coats over their black suits, hopped off their motorcycles and scurried toward the hospital entrance. One of the fellows braced against the door forcing it open. They entered the hospital. The beasts were unleashed. The power of their bare hand was too much for any human being, for what they did they knew it had pierced the heart of heaven. Within the grasp of their palms they preyed upon everyone in their path. The body parts of pregnant women, old folks, doctors, and nurses scattered on the floor, their lives snatched away like well-fed bears playing with salmon.

The men scanned rooms, bathrooms, and the kitchen. They entered a darkroom. When their eyes adjusted they spotted a bed at the center of the room, a girl crumpled in bed groaning in agony. That didn't deter them from inflicting more pain. The girl screamed until her voice faded, gagging for air until her lungs collapsed. Two of the men moved towards an open window at the far side of the room. They stared at a car parked a few feet away from the hospital.

The car's headlights suddenly flicked on, almost blinding the two fellows who used their hands to push away the lights.

Inside of the car, a younger Father Johnson, early thirties, wearing a priest outfit, was the driver.

"Father Andrew," he said. "Which of these foot rests is the accelerator?" Father Andrew, mid-twenties, wearing a similar outfit to Father Johnson, sat in the backseat cuddling an identical twin, newborn. One of the babies thundered a high frequency squeak and shattered the car windshield; from the eyes of the other baby blood trickled.

"Father Johnson, it's God's will," said Father Andrew. "Close yer eyes and press down on anything that set the car forwards." Father Johnson closed his eyes and smashed his foot against a pedal, setting the car in rapid motion. Outside the hospital, a thunderous boom echoed as the men plunged through the walls and windows. Rubble heaped as concrete and steel crumpled like the aftermath of an earthquake. The men seemed unharmed and dashed out of the way as they spotted a car hurling toward them, in reverse. The car stopped then swerved away in the opposite direction.

Advancing towards the car the men sprinted as fast as their legs allowed, until they reached the parking lot. The car retreated further and further. In the parking lot they found their bikes' tires all punctured. The men kicked and punched their useless machines. With teeth grinding and hatred bubbling in their heart, only if they could get a hold of those in that wretched car, all their hard work seemed to be in vein. What they'd come for now slipped away into the desolated countryside of Jamaica. But the stories in their eyes had just begun. For Fathers Andrew and Johnson had no idea what they got themselves into.

The plane experienced extreme turbulence, bumping father Andrew out of the past. He shuffled in his seat, looking out of his mind. The years had worn him. Things he used to do he'd no interest for anymore, he'd served his purpose, but his spirit remained to guide Detective Mullson.

Mullson thought long and hard about the words lingering in his head. Father Andrew's conversation was blurry, just like the demon of Mullson's past that resurfaced a few weeks ago, before he set out across Africa to meet his brother Daniel. The pair had always been close, they had similar taste and hobbies, felt each other's pain, after all they're the same person. Identical except for a secret each carried, but unaware of.

"The child who cries blood?" said Detective Mullson, glancing at Father Andrew wryly, from the corner of an eye.

"Believe it my son. Yer destiny shall come to light," said Father Andrew, in a hushed voice.

Detective Mullson was in a crunch. He felt awkward and was not sure what to believe. Yet he had no doubts of all the possibilities from things he'd encountered and what his brother had told.

"Are you afraid of the Congo, Father?" he said.

"Afraid of the Congo," said Father Andrew. "Afraid of…" He chuckled as he sorted through his cranium. "Some enjoy the wonder, others are petrified by it," Father Andrew continued, sounding a little nervous.

"I will stick to the Chinese stuff," said Detective Mullson. "Perfect peace of mind is a balance between good and evil. One cannot exist without the other, something like that."

Father Andrew sighed. "Do you believe in transcendentalism?"

Nina, after snatching a bottle of champagne from her trolley, went and stood by the gentleman she'd been stalking, mentally. Every time she passed his seat her knees felt as if they were about to give way. Butterflies rumbled in her tummy. Electricity ran throughout her body, making her clit vibrate, like a disturbed rattle snake. Nina got moist— very, very moist. She urged for a big one, the more she thought about him— oh yeah baby. If only she could get him in the bathroom to bang the hell out of him.

"Hello sir," she said, to Mullson, interrupting. "Anything special?"

"Both of us could use a shot of that," Father Andrew told Nina, referring to the champagne.

Nina ignored Father Andrew's request. She only seemed interested in Mullson and asked him again, "Sir, do you want anything?"

"A drink of water please," Mullson answered her. "Father Andrew also needs a drink."

"You could have both," she said, in a sexy tone. "One is on me." Nina headed towards the back of the plane. A dirty grin flashed across her face as she licked her lips and closed her eyes. "What a handsome weirdo," she said to herself.

The moment Nina exited first class the deranged man preyed upon her. He shoved a nail clipper against her throat and held her hostage with the sharp edge of the filing component.

Passengers clinched to their seats.

Along with his hostage the deranged man moved towards the front of the plane. Goosebumps flooded his arms as fear rushed throughout his veins.

"They're here!" he roared.

Other passengers were worried that the lunatic would harm Nina; nobody was interested in what he was saying.

In the lower compartment personal belongings scattered as if someone was searching luggage, the stench of rotten meat filled the air. A faint laughter echoed from the midst of the room. Wrath darted from behind a pile of clothes. He was wearing a khaki outfit, Rastafarian hat and a pair of sunglasses. His face was still blackened from the roast, pus gushed from holes at the side of his jaws. Wrath spotted a mp3 player on the floor, he jammed the headphone in his ears then hit play.

"SEX MUST REWIND, IT IS SO FINE…" he sang along to a song by Masta Recka and Jeano. "Something smells funky," he blurted, sniffing his way to oversized panties lying on the floor. He picked up the drawers and rubbed them against his face, picturing himself with a lightly dressed female who pulled out his penis and forced it in her mouth, swallowing it halfway and at times licking it like a lollipop. Wrath got more than his money's worth. Laughing out of control he blew a fart that had him check the rear of his pants.

The deranged man dragged Nina towards the front of the plane. She kicked and tossed her hands about, but he kept poking the clipper further into her neck, subsequently calming her. Passengers sat in their seats and hoped for the best.

Detective Mullson was the only one to get up; he stood in the path of the man who came lunging into first-class. But the fellow made up his mind he wouldn't be stopped. He had a message to deliver and it needed to be heard. The more attention he got the merrier, for unpleasant things were about to happen to this world. God had sent him to help save humankind, as if anyone would ever believe such nonsense.

Welcome to Earth, for today was not the day to mess with Trevor Mullson who had enough with people taking advantage of the weak, and worst, no regard for the laws he fought to protect. He stared the fellow in the eyes and tried to figure the next move, from the man's breathing patterns to the sweat penetrating the forehead, nothing went unnoticed.

The man's heart skipped a beat as he stared back into Mullson's cold eyes; somehow he figured his opponent was special, but a little confused. He ventured deep into Mullson's soul and realized mankind's chance against the enemies had improved, a slim chance indeed. The dark side had cast the spell of doom on whom Engulf thought was a common man to carry out his bidden — Daniel will never or cannot be controlled, just as Mullson's blood will always be feared. Inching closer towards Mullson the man braced against Nina's back.

"Don't let me!" he said to Mullson, sounding desperate. He flung Nina to the floor then positioned a karate pose, boastfully exhibiting his quick hands, too swift for any human to observe other than flashes of blurriness.

This was Mullson's first test, but he had no idea. He tried to focus on the hands that had him dizzy. Pretending to be unimpressed, he tossed a kick that connected the man in the throat. With blood spraying from his mouth, the deranged man went flying in the opposite direction. Two men got up and apprehended the unconscious fellow. The echo of claps filled the air. Nina showed her gratitude with a quick kiss to Mullson's lips.

"Thank you," said Mullson, to the cheerful passengers, heading back to his seat. "Thank you."

Father Andrew didn't seem thrilled. "The war is already started," he told Mullson.

Mullson had begun to wonder if Father Andrew was also missing a screw. He blamed himself for falling for some of the old man antics. How could such an educated man like himself fall for religious mumbo-jumbo? Damn Mullson, you should know better.

Little did he know Engulf was already scouting out a single family house somewhere in Long Island, New York. As dawn descended he focused on the mailbox at the front of nine hundred and ninety-nine Storehill Drive, a black Expedition in the driveway, and a window located on the second floor. Not that it mattered, for Mullson had never met Engulf. Why Engulf had such great interest in the Mullson brothers put the whole family in jeopardy.

CHAPTER 3

M ullson and other passengers had already boarded their connecting flight in Europe and were well on their way to America. The wind was calm throughout the night. Dawn had come and gone. The plane drew closer to the East coast of the United States. Seagulls hovering over the Hudson River increased in large numbers closer to New York, where an atmosphere of gloom descended on the crowded city below. Smoke plummeted from chimneys towering above the Tri-State, even more so along the New Jersey turnpike.

Inside first-class, Father Andrew and Detective Mullson continued to sit next to each other. "You need to pay closer attention," Father Andrew advised Mullson, his cold eyes hadn't blinked for the past few minutes.

"So what about this transcend stuff?" said Mullson, trying to reflect back on an earlier topic.

Again, the Jeft couple sat across from Mullson. Mr. Jeft tried his best to fit his long frame into his seat as he took a quick snooze. Mrs. Jeft regretted listening to

Mullson's conversation and wished she'd followed her husband's opinion, not to mingle around. A doubt in her mind had her panicking, the fact she couldn't figure who Mullson was talking with had begun to take a toll on her already failing health. A few years back she'd suffered a stroke-- a massive attack that left her right side paralyzed and impaired her vision. With vigorous therapy her health had improved, but she never fully recovered. Mrs. Jeft looked at Detective Mullson; she smiled when he turned and glanced at her.

"We heard that story before," she said, using an elbow to jab her husband in the side. "Haven't we sweetheart?"

Mr. Jeft jumped and grabbed his rib cage. "Honey, come on," he said. "Told you to leave that stuff alone."

"But Conrad said its okay," she reminded her husband.

"Who is Conrad?" Detective Mullson asked the woman.

"Our son," she said, elbowing her husband again. "Right sweetheart."

"Yes, honey," Mr. Jeft answered under his breath.

"Our son is a proud police officer at the John F. Kennedy Airport," said the woman, to Mullson. She handed him a business card. "This is our number, you could call us. Do you mind if I ask you one more question?"

"Honey?" said her husband, in disapproval.

"What?" she answered.

"It's okay," Mullson told her.

"Are you having problems with women?" she blurted to Mullson.

Detective Mullson smiled. "Not quite," he assured her.

"Why are you talking to yourself?" She asked Mullson.

Father Andrew laughed, so did Mullson who had no clue what was happening and thought the old lady had trouble with her eyesight. Mullson found the couple somewhat confusing, towards him they were polite, yet acted as if Father Andrew was invisible, kind of weird, he thought. He turned and glanced at the old textbook Father Andrew had being skimming through.

"If the soul tricks the body" Father Andrew whispered to himself, "the enemy will rest in peace."

"What about people who die accidentally," said Mullson to Father Andrew, after recalling a dream. "Can they come back to haunt us?"

Father Andrew stared at the book and sensed something was wrong, his emotions seemingly got the best of him, and he no longer felt connected to life. "Maybe," he managed a whisper.

"Ladies and gentlemen," the Captain voice echoed over the intercom. "It's a wonderful day in New York City."

Emptiness consumed Father Andrew's thoughts, like a lone star in the galaxy his mind wandered. It was close to two years since he stood on top of a towering building somewhere in the heart of New York City and fought a raging storm. The demon from within had confronted him, but he stood his ground with faith in the God he trusted. As a priest he was extraordinary skilled in an ancient language of anti-curse, uttering strange words that rattled the nerves of the dead. He held a metal cross above his head that attracted a bolt of lightning, he shook out of control. What appeared to be a phantom leaped out of his body and hovered in midair — hundreds of feet above the road. The ghostly figure was a spitting image of Father Andrew. It stood and watched as he chanted, "The work of God is stronger than evil!"

The plane's wings shifted and resisted against a sudden rush of wind, slowing as it approached New York City. As the plane began its descent, Mullson looked out the window and poked a piece of gum into his mouth. He could see the tops of skyscrapers, the Statue of Liberty, and the crammed streets below. The plane took a sharp turn and aligned with a runaway at John F. Kennedy Airport. The landing gear popped from the belly, at the edge of the wings the brake flaps slid out. Darting along, the wheels thundered against the pavement before squeaking to a halt.

As soon as Mullson stepped inside the arrival building a blast of cold air hit his face. He hurried along a passageway until he reached a room that eventually was packed with people. He joined the line for U.S citizens and handed his passport to a clean shaven gentleman who took it and smiled.

The man skimmed through and stamped across a clean page, before handing it back. "Have a good day, Detective Mullson," he said.

Mullson opened his carryon and shoved the passport into a side compartment. "Thank you."

By the time he left customs Mullson was already under the radar, a security officer followed his every move, staying a good pace back. Scurrying towards baggage claim Mullson glanced over his shoulder and wondered where Father Andrew went, he hopped onto an escalator that took him down to a large open area where weary passengers stood waiting at a conveyer belt spinning with luggage, hauling off their belongings when spotted. The officer edged closer and closer to Mullson who had no clue of the man's intention. He finally spotted him and wondered if he was being tailed; because of recent threats facing the airport he let the thought slide.

Mullson grabbed his luggage and dashed towards the exit on the opposite side of the room. The officer went to the door and glanced at Mullson, from his pocket he retrieved his cellphone and sent a text: He's back.

A docile German shepherd who'd being lying peace-
fully on the floor jumped and tugged to be set free. With
all his might Jeft held onto to the leash while his partner
Barton stood over a piece of luggage, both men were in
their late thirties. Barton stooped and ripped the luggage
open. The 20-month-old K9 finally broke loose and
sprinted away. Both officers gave chase, as fast as their
legs could carry them. People ran and screamed as they
spotted the furious dog. He dashed into a plane and
pounced upon the seat where Detective Mullson had sat
earlier. Jeft and Barton tumbled in and stood gasping for
air. Their hearts raced, sweat dripped from their foreheads, itchiness tickled their legs.

The dog rushed to the back of the plane, echoed a
bark, dived over a trolley and entered the galley. After
sensing something in the darkness, with killer instincts he
preyed upon the unknown. His ninety pounds of raw
muscle was no match for whatever was inside that room,
for as soon as he entered his body got tossed in the
opposite direction, landing where Jeft and Barton stood,
all the way to first class.

Both men's hearts raced even more as fear spread
through their veins. With their fingers twitching for the
slightest of movement, they ripped their gun from its
holsters and aimed. Jeft strode silently toward the back of
the plane while Barton stood over the badly hurt canine.
Jeft shoved the trolley out of the way and continued to

scan his surroundings, drawing closer to the galley, he entered. Barton stooped. "Jeft," he said.

"I'm listening," Jeft answered, from the midst of the galley.

"Be careful."

"I'll be okay Sam."

Barton pickup his radio and yelled, "We have an emergency aboard plane. Canine down. Please send reinforcement."

The lights flickered, darkness followed.

"Jeft!" Barton bellowed. "Jeft! Are you okay?" Hidden by the darkness someone exited the galley, Barton shined his flashlight and spotted the name JEFT across the chest of a figure standing tall. Just as the plane regained power a human head propelled forward and knocked Barton off his feet.

Outside, people crammed the sidewalk waiting to enter taxis, their cars, or other transportations available. Detective Mullson walked back and forth, glanced at his cellphone to check the time, gazed at oncoming traffic stopping to pick up passengers. In the distance he spotted a black Ford Expedition approaching, a smile flashed across his face as he rushed and retrieved his luggage. A beautiful girl with dimpled cheeks came out and hugged him.

"Miss Anna, how ya doing?" he said.

"I'm fine dad, how was your trip?" she said.

"Well," he said hesitantly, "we'll talk later."

Mullson hurriedly tossed his luggage into the back of the SUV; as they pulled out of the airport they spotted helicopters hovering above, NYPD, and fire rescue ambulances and trucks from Engine CO 29, heading the opposite direction, toward the arrival ramp.

NYPD officers rushed into the plane and found a man, a head, and a dog, all confirmed dead. At the back of the plane an officer discovered a decapitated body, stripped of clothing. A white male and a black female, wearing FBI jackets, entered. The man is Agent Hill, about forty-two. He walked with a certain swagger that commanded attention.

"Listen up boys," he said. "I'll take it from here." The woman is Agent McKoy, early thirties, with a pretty face and a gorgeous body.

"Someone is pissed off," she said, after observing the scene.

"Wonder what provoked him?" said Agent Hill, sounding confident.

"Or her," Agent McKoy added.

A white male, about mid-forties, entered. He sported black dress pants and a white dress shirt unbuttoned and revealing a pink undershirt. He had a cellphone in one hand and a paper bag containing food in the other. Jack flashed his badge before Agent Hill's face.

"Just the man I don't want to see," he said with an Italian accent.

Agent Hill retaliated with a mean look across his face.

Agent McKoy stared at them and shook her head.

Agent Hill and Jack forced an innocent smile.

Detective Jack, after squeezing by Agent Hill, went and stooped over the canine; he ripped the bag open and stuffed a hot dog in his mouth, afterwards, dialed his cellphone. Agent Hill glanced at Jeft's head in a bag resting on a nearby seat.

"Hope you and Mullson don't take matters into your own hands," Hill warned.

"What do you know about us?" asked Jack, sounding a little edgy.

"Off the record," said Agent Hill, looking over his shoulder. "You two are a menace to society. More like the devil's advocate."

"Somebody's got to do your job," Jack blurted, to Agent Hill. "Better watch your wife."

"Jack?" said Agent McKoy, in disapproval.

"I know you like me," said Jack, flirting with her. "But I'm not ready for a serious rejection-ship, gives me sometime sweetheart." Even though she pretended not to give in, Agent McKoy had begun to fall for Jack more than ever, his sexy accents, the way he put a smile in her heart, his crazy words.

The very words that annoyed Agent Hill who stood grinding his teeth and clinching his fists, "You arrogant bastard!" he shouted at Jack.

"Okay," said McKoy, "enough."

"I'm going to give my partner a call," Jack told McKoy, teasingly. "Hope you're not jealous."

As the evening progressed, traffic was moving bumper to bumper for miles, nothing unusual during rush hour on any New York City street. Heading east on I-495, a black Expedition sandwiched front and back between two armored trucks had been trying to make a move. As soon as other cars spotted the indicator they raced to narrow the gap.

Inside the SUV Anna Mullson glanced left and spotted a car, she tried to swing right but she had no way out as they approached exit 41S, about a mile ahead. Anna was in her early twenties, with hair hanging to her shoulder, perfectly aligned teeth. Yet not many guys were willing to date her. Not that anything was wrong with her. They were afraid of what she had; the bully sitting at the front passenger seat. Detective Mullson's reputation spread throughout the Tri-state: hard criminals feared him for his ruggedness; Anna's wannabe boyfriends never got the guts to face him. Deep down Mullson had the heart of a baby, but continued to play tough.

Dimples sunk in Anna's cheeks as she smiled off the frustration built up inside. Those bastards kept her trapped. She thought about tunneling her way to the next lane, luckily the crawling of traffic bought her more time, so her mind hadn't been freaking about missing her exit. She flicked on a pair of sunglasses she retrieved from a storage compartment and focused on the armored truck ahead. The truck seemingly underwent some form of x-rays, as if penetrated by Anna's powerful eyes, a computer projection revealed two skeletons at the back; they appeared to be engaged in some form of unusual activity. Anna took off her sunglasses and everything was back to normal.

"Dad," she said.

All sorts of things scattered in Mullson's brain, he braced against his seat, almost pushing it all the way back. The long journey had begun to take a toll on him. "Yes, Miss Anna," he answered.

She gave him the sunglasses. "That's your Father's Day gift," she said. "It's only ten days late." Mullson was more than happy for the pair of sunglasses and slapped them on to block the sun pouring through the front windshield.

"Holy crop," he said, almost jumping out of his seat. "Where did you get this?"

"Just enjoy your gift," said Anna, with a smirked across her face.

Mullson focused on the armored truck ahead; he saw an image of two skeletons at the back of the truck — one standing, the other resting both knees on the floor. The skeleton with knees resting on the floor moved the head region back and forth at the waistline of the standing skeleton. The first thing that flashed across Mullson's mind: what on earth are they doing? He'd now witnessed the future of spyware — a dirty business, real dirty.

Anna spotted the sign that read: Exit 41S.

"It's time," she said.

Mullson continued to focus on the freak show ahead.

"Take the other exit," he suggested.

Anna plowed her way to the right lane then made a sharp turn onto exit 41S. "Sorry," she teased.

The armored truck continued on further south. Inside the back of the truck a security guard stood tall with a wrenched facial expression. He closed his eyes and groaned. "Good job honey."

"This is a hard one," a male voice echoed. Looking down, another male guard was resting on his knees sewing his comrade's zipper; he moved his head back and forth to avoid the needle.

CHAPTER 4

The sun had begun to fade as Anna cruised along route 107, a small town near Broadway mall, somewhere in Hicksville. Trees towering on both sides of the street hid most of the houses. Less than two miles away stood Old Westbury College and a short distance after C.W. Post University. College students gave this tiny town levity. Most of the rich folks in Old Westbury were not happy about students invading their town, they loved it the way it used to be, quiet, more wooded, and not so friendly. The trees were breathtaking, especially during the fall when their leaves changed from green to yellow, and finally reddish-brown. The residents in this sophisticated area seemed to be handpicked, except for Mullson and a few other minorities who got tossed in to deaden the racial stigma that taunted the area awhile back.

Detective Mullson had begun to doze when his cell-phone vibrated. "Hello," he said, after pressing the answer key. "Mullson speaking. Wait a minute, slow down a little. What yuh mean? I'll call yuh later."

Anna angled the Expedition along a familiar side street barely visible from the main road, hidden among the shrubs and trees. From the corner of her eye she glanced at her dad and could tell he was worried; she waited for him to say something, but he didn't. "So what's that about?" she finally asked.

"Not sure," said Detective Mullson, using a hand to pull on his chin. "I'll find out later. Hmm... strange."

"Dad, what's wrong?"

Something about that priest is not adding up? A thought kept hopping around in Mullson's head, he got so caught up he didn't even hear his daughter.
"So, how was it?" Anna continued.

"Things never worked out," he said. "My brother gave me his word. That's not like him for not showing up."

"Here we go again," said Anna, slowing as she approached nine hundred and ninety-nine Storehill Drive, "Always taking up for your people. Uncle Daniel is only human. What is he doing in the Congo to begin with?"

Father Andrew had being roaming around New York City, sometimes more than one place at a time, like what was happening at the 96 Street and the 125 Street train terminals. At 96 Street, by a pay phone, he stood and glanced at a man in a white suit standing at the edge of the uptown platform. Father Andrew drifted toward the yellow line and placed a hand on the man's shoulder.

Further inside the tunnel a train accelerated towards the uptown platform.

The man turned and stared at the rest of commuters. Suddenly a cool evening breeze sent shivers down his spine. He trembled a bit as he observed the station for the last time. His clothes became reddened, almost as if blood was gushing through his pores.

Meanwhile, at the 125 Street Station, about four stops further uptown from 96 Street, Father Andrew was also at the edge of the platform with a hand resting on the shoulder of a gentleman wearing a black outfit. The man crossed beyond the yellow line then stared at the crowd, people wondered what his intention was. The sounds of a train squealed in the distance — an uptown train approaching at high speed drew closer. "I'll save the God in you," said Father Andrew. "But the devil has to go!"

At 96 Street Station Father Andrew watched as the train hit the fellow in the white suit, scattering body parts in all directions. The wheels of the train squeaked, fire sparked as metal rubbed, the sudden pull on the emergency brakes sent people flying as the No.5 tumbled to a halt.

Back in Long Island a Ford Expedition turned onto the driveway of nine hundred and ninety-nine Storehill Drive and parked before the garage. Inside the SUV the radio lowered in the background, Anna and Detective Mullson unbuckled their seatbelts.

"Hope mom is happy," she said.

Mullson sighed, "Been awhile. Think it will work? Hold for a minute." Detective Mullson wound the knob right and turned up the volume.

The Reporter's voice echoed, "At about five-thirty in the evening two men committed suicide at two separate New York City Subway Stations."

"This is a crazy world," Anna gave out.

"Tell me about it."

Next door a dove perched on a statue of the Virgin Mary. "That's a sign of good luck," said Anna, pointing at the dove.

"I could use some of that," Mullson admitted.

They got out of the vehicle and hauled themselves up a few steps to get to the front patio. Anna searched a bundle of keys she whisked from her pocketbook, inserted one into the front door and turned the knob.

She entered the living room and held the door open as her father shuffled by with his luggage. Detective Mullson placed his belonging at the foot of the stairs leading to the upper floor, at a corner not blocking the path.

Wall grilles and wall plaques crafted from wrought iron, with patterns of fleur-de-lis, hung on bare wall space in the living room. Ceramic tiles sporting lovely fleur-de-lis designs bordered the fireplace opposite the staircase, adding brightness and an inviting feel to the room. Throw Pillows cuddled the sofa and loveseat, a sixty-inch television on an entertainment unit placed against the wall was on, at the center stood a cocktail table with shaped legs and scrolled details, made of stone with the warmth of a copper-brown finish.

Inside the kitchen Magarette Mullson listened to the television in the backdrop. Looking like a goddess in a teal dress hugging her curvy configuration, the one she ordered online and got two days ago. She stood by the gas range preparing ginger shrimp stir-fry and vegetable fried rice. Already the radiating aroma had their mouths watering.

Anna went and threw her arms around her mother, squeezing her gently. "Hi mom," she said. "Dad is here."

"Hi baby," said Magarette to Anna, with a light Jamaican accent.

From the dining room Detective Mullson entered the kitchen.

"Hi honey," he said to Magarette, "your husband is home."

Magarette yanked the cover off a pot and stirred the rice she'd been slow cooking, facing away the whole time. Her facial expression changed from the sweet soul she was to looking all wretched with her eyes popping out. "Two long months and one postcard," she said, in a bitter tone, pretending not to be happy to see the man that made her heart flutter and who threatened to press charges against her for stealing his heart when they'd first met. "That's what you call love?"

Detective Mullson inched closer to his wife, cautiously. "Honey," he said, pulling on his chin. "You know how the job is. I'm planning for an early retirement… I'll give Jack a call."

"If you guys need me I'll be upstairs," said Anna, scurrying away.

"Bye darling," said her parents, they stood looking as she dashed through the living room and towards the stairway that led to her room. "See you at dinner," Mrs. Mullson added. She turned off the stove. "Jack can wait until tomorrow," she told Trevor.

On the second floor, Anna came to a door which stood slightly ajar; she pushed the door and entered her room. Inside the room, posters of various fashion models cluttered the walls, soft music, playing at a moderate level, filled the air. Stuffed animals and pillows bundled at the head of her bed, a dresser resting in one corner was packed with colognes, lotions, and makeup. Anna shuffled towards a nightstand and snatched a cordless phone from its base then went and stood by the window facing the front yard.

Mullson had promised Father Andrew a visit sometime tonight, ten o' clock to be exact. He thought about telling his wife, but decided to wait until later. By the kitchen sink he went and adjusted the faucet until the water felt pleasing, before rinsing away the lather from his hands, and used a piece of paper towel he ripped from the holder to wipe them dry.

Mrs. Mullson skimmed through the refrigerator. "So what's the plan for tonight, Mister Busy?" she asked.

Detective Mullson jiggled his bum and twirled his waist, slowly, as he unleashed his freakiness to lure his wife who had begun to drift into a fantasy. By the look on her face he figured she was getting wet, and he kept pressing. Mullson came towards her and removed his shirt, exposing his muscular chest and rock hard abs. "After my meeting," he teased, "a whole bunch of action, baby."

Before she got a chance to oppose him, he grabbed her and forced his chest against her back, between finger and thumb he tweaked her nipples gently, until they became hard and erect.

At first Mrs. Mullson wanted to push his hands away, but didn't, especially after an electrifying sensation started to rush from her breasts to her clit, she turned and faced him, they kissed each other on the lips, slowly, then randomly on the neck, chest, breast, like there was no tomorrow.

CHAPTER 5

In the Bronx the night got extraordinarily cold for this time of year, but nobody seemed to be complaining, for it had to be better than fans rushing the hot summer air against the body. Other than that, residents went about without noticing unusual activity at the Catholic Church bordered by Eastchester Road, Mickle Avenue, and Adee Avenue. The church, with stained-glass designs filled where red-brick didn't occupy, towered high above the surrounding houses that stood about three stories. Drives and parking spaces carved in a well maintained grass lawn that spread throughout the churchyard, a variety of tulips, roses, and others flowers scattered closer to the hedges.

A cat that had been scanning the yard all day kept checking a hole where a rat dodged earlier, finally got distracted by strange men on the outskirts glancing at the cross above the church's steeple. Several of the men sprinted forward and jumped to hurl their bodies above the ten foot fence; they almost succeeded if it wasn't for the cat who thundered a purr and curled up as they approached.

From in the church Father Andrew glanced at his unwelcome guests as they darted away. Something or someone made them gallop away. What could have spooked them? This he needed to know to protect Detective Mullson. In the meantime he prayed for mankind, for Mullson and his family, for the people living in the community. He wished Mullson a safe journey in hope he arrives before the angel of darkness returns.

Later in the night, for hours, there was not a single human roaming the street. A mysterious figure slithering along Adee Avenue came and stood at a corner opposite the church, about thirty meters away. He observed every movement, like the ruffling of tree branches by the unusual icy wind, shadows creeping about in the churchyard, a cat crunched to attack a mouse. The glowing of the moon, after slipping from behind a dark cloud, offered less coverage as the thing unblended with the darkness. The air rushing across his over six foot frame didn't prevent his ears from twitching at the sounds of a clock echoing from within the depths of the church, inaudible for any human from where he stood. He tipped back his head and peered at the cross towering above the roof of the church, and spotted a crow perching.

From inside the church Father Andrew kept a close eye on the creature. Something is preventing him from coming to snatch away the book, the thought occurred to him. The only thing he spotted in the churchyard for the past days was a stray cat.

"Are they afraid of the cat?" he whispered. In the backdrop, the silence was broken by the revving of an engine and the squeaking of tires against pavement. The man seemed startled as a silver Porsche 911 Carrera swerved towards him; the car was moving at top speed all the way to the corner of Adee Avenue. The headlights revealed the man to be Engulf. Mullson spotted him and continued to slam on the brakes, but it was useless.

The crow thundered a squawk as the Porsche collided with Engulf.

Detective Mullson had the life knocked out of his body, against a deployed airbag his face rested, with a cold wind rushing across his body his mind drifted to the other side.

Inside the church, lights dimmed high above from its arching ceiling, rows of benches aligned equally distant. On the floor, at the middle of the church, Detective Mullson's unconscious body rested. Father Andrew, carrying a jar of water, entered from a rear door. He hurried to the center of the church and splashed the water against Mullson's face. Mullson opened his eyes and tried to focus on the lights above.

"Where am I?" he said.

"Don't worry," Father Andrew replied. "You're safe now."

"My car?"

"Yer car is perfectly fine."

A clock located high on the wall striked as Mullson hustled to his feet; the time read ten o' clock.
"It's very important to follow time," Father Andrew continued.

"Thought I was on point," said Mullson, looking at the clock.

With fury fuming in his heart Father Andrew headed back toward the rear door he'd come from earlier. In his mind Mullson had broken the first rule — the most important one.
"If you want to survive I suggest you do exactly what I say," he warned. The only thing Mullson could do was watch as the old man walked away.

"Are you implying that punctuality is a bad thing?" he asked.

"Ten o'clock means, exactly that," said Father Andrew, almost reaching the rear door.

"Is he dead?" said Mullson, after summing up the courage.

Father Andrew, facing away, came to a standstill. "Sometimes what we see," he said, "is what we should not."

"Is he dead?" Mullson bellowed.

"Please excuse yourself Detective Mullson!" Father Andrew snarled, stretching for the knob, he shoved the door and exited.

The minute Mullson got to his car he scanned every inch of his surroundings, but he didn't find any sign of the man he swore he'd hit — the one who disappeared within the strangeness of the night, without even spilling a drop of blood. He inspected the car over and over, and found nothing unusual.

On the other side of town, truckers descended upon an imperiled neighborhood after a long trip to one of New York's largest fish markets. Hunts Point flourished from the fish business. Other than the fish market, there was not much to see. On the outskirts, surrounded by rundown buildings, drug dealers and prostitutes roamed the streets.

Pimps staked out their prey, every dollar counted in this game of cat and mouse, and no bitch escaped their grasp. Lightly dressed ladies stood on the corner slaving for a living, allowing customers to sneak a peek at their overused packages – fishy, with a dash of powder to freshen up. Police cars crept about the dark streets, lights flashing as they zoomed up and down, deterring drivers who'd stop to talk to women on almost every other corner.

In the distance, a motorcycle approached. A lightly dressed lady spotted the motorcycle slowing and walked forward. The rider, face concealed by a helmet, sat on the bike and waited as the woman came and stood close by. They talked briskly; she pointed him to an abandoned building where he hid the bike at the side of the house and followed her up a flight of stairs, leading to the main door. She braced against the door, the hinges squeaked as the door swung open, they entered a dark hallway where a musky scent of mold and dust cluttered the air and made the woman spray a few sneezes.

Boots and heels pounded against the wooden stair-way, broken in a few areas. The building trembled beneath their feet. The lady guided the stranger to a room on the third floor and wasted no time as she used her lighter and lit a candle she placed at the center of the empty room; near the sole window where the moon light got reflected by a barrier of dust collected over the years, she brushed off a deflated air bed and forced the man to lie on his back. Cobwebs entangled the ceiling and other areas that were left undisturbed.

The stranger smacked the lady on her butt, repeatedly till she moaned out in pleasure.

"It's your time baby," his voice echoed. "Just make it smooth." She slid down his zipper and sat on something, large, her eyes widened with excitement as she forced it into her wet cunny. Every untouched spot was finally reached by the thick long dick the stranger possessed. Not that she planned to enjoy the show, only for the money, but she got carried away, fulfilling her deepest fantasy as she indulged in sex beyond her wildest imagination. Little did she know the creature lurking under the helmet was thirsty for life, for anything that comforted the desire of his maker, for a taste of the hot blood gushing through her veins — he resisted all the temptations, but the maker reached out — and the dark-side took control of his body.

The woman loved the way she had the stranger screaming for more, doubling the pace in an effort to leave a mark on his dick, she guaranteed him a night he'd never forget while hoping he'd return. Thirty minutes had come and gone, yet she didn't stop, as she did on countless occasions. She now broke the first rule of engagement — and sensed her pimp was already on his way to deal her justice — but she'd no intention of stopping now. Her body began to shake out of control. She'd never felt like this before, the way her vagina contracted as secretion sprayed out.

The man continued to wail, the lady had being doing her best to please him, at first he wanted it and was amazed when she sat on the whole thing, as if he had a toothpick down there. The pain became overbearing. The headache seemed to trouble him more during times of happiness; he yanked off his helmet and tossed it aside.

The sex ended abruptly as the woman stared at his charred face, at first she tried to yell but she couldn't, and when she finally did, a shrilling sound filled the air as she screamed her soul out.

Pimps heard the ruckus and rushed in the direction from where it came, springing with all their might they reached the building and busted through the front gate, the sounds of glass shattering had them looking up at a third floor window where a female head had crashed through and landed on the street below.

About two hours later, in Manhattan, outside of Marco's Sport's Bar, located on the first floor of a high-rise building, a group of bikers were hanging out smoking and drinking; most of them stood blocking the entrance as people squeezed their way to the bar, or to their apartments above.

Residents feared the worst as gang bangers began to invade their neighborhood. To some the bikers were rowdy and disgusting, people kept calling the police but nothing was done to remedy the situation. Quite a few residents prayed for the day when those bastards would get their share of the pie they'd being dishing for way too long.

Inside the bar, colorful lights dazzled, on a small stage musicians blew saxophones and strummed guitars. Maxine, an attractive young lady in a short skirt, sleeveless top, and boots just below the knees, danced to the sweet melodies. At the counter, Detective Mullson sat and held his head, all night he'd been trying to shun Father Andrew's voice, especially the words: Sometimes what we see, is what we should not. "Bullshit!" he bellowed, slamming his palm against the counter.

At fifty-five years old the bartender had been here for the past decade, as the years shredded, his blonde hair was almost white, but nothing seemed to slow him. Family operated, his club had a fair share of gangsters, Mafia, and pimps— he'd seen it all. He came and stood by Mullson. "Mullson," said Marco, with a strong Italian accent. "Are you okay?"

"I'll be alright," said Mullson. "Just need a few minutes to clear my head."

Jack, wearing a white suit, holding an unlit cigar in one hand, entered and began to stare at Maxine as she passed him on her way out. He turned and smiled, after glancing at her ass — "If I could get a hold of that strong booty," he thought to himself, "damn she's fine as a…"

"Stop watching my ass you pervert!" Maxine said with a coarse voice, but to herself she thought, oh my God, that white suit is the bomb.

"Holy crop," said a confused Jack, scurrying towards Detective Mullson. He quickly erased all the dirty thoughts lingering in his head. He'd fallen for Maxine's strong legs and thick body, damn, he still can't believe she's a man. "What's up partner," he teased Mullson, "you look like a bum. Did the Motherland chew you up and spit you out?"

"What's up Detective Jack, ass?" said Mullson mockingly.

"Jack for you mister," said Jack jokingly.

"You guys haven't changed one bit," said Marco, retrieving a half full glass from Mullson.

"What's up uncle?" Jack greeted Marco. "Give me some of what Mullson is drinking. Looks like some strong shit."

Marco handed him a glass of what Jack thought to be brandy. Jack took a sip and immediately spit the contents back into the glass, slamming it on the counter.

"You asked for it," Mullson teased.

"Apple Juice is for babies," Jack blurted. "I need something more manly." He dipped into his jacket pocket and pulled out some photos. Detective Mullson skimmed through the photos Jack handed him.

"Who's the guy without the head?" he asked Jack.

"Jeft," said Jack. "He used to work at JFK. Both of his partners got killed."

Mullson ran a hand across his chin. "Jeft," he said, shuffling his brain to where he'd heard the name. "Jeft. Conrad Jeft?"

"You knew him?" Jack asked.

"Long story," said Mullson.

"What about the others?"

"Sam Barton and K," said Jack, almost as if nothing happened.

"Where is Kay?" said Mullson.

"K as in K9," Jack replied.

Marco came over and glanced at a picture. "What kind of person kills a dog?" he asked.

Outside the bar, the bikers continued to hangout. As the night progressed the alcohol had began to poison their minds, even more. An old fellow using a rod to find his way around walked towards the rowdy bunch and slammed into a motorcycle. A biker spotted the man and came towards him; swinging his foot he connected the man in the buttocks, hurling the blind fellow through the air. The man got up and dashed down the street, bumping into the unknown as he desperately tried to save his life.

Inside Marco's Sport's Bar, the crowd began to vanish; the musicians packed away their gear, Detective Mullson handed Jack a business card.

"They seem like nice folks," he said. "We could pay them a visit tomorrow."

"Lets call it a night," Jack advised Mullson. "See you later uncle," he waved goodbye to Marco.

"Goodnight Uncle Marco," said Mullson, waving.

"Keep out of trouble you two," Marco warned, waving back as they exited.

The instant Jack and Mullson stepped outside they got confronted by the biker who'd earlier kicked the blind fellow in the buttocks. Mullson head-butted his opponent and left him in a bloody mess. The rest of bikers rushed towards Mullson and Jack — they kicked, punched, and slapped.

The bikers gained an early advantage with their numbers.

Detective Mullson's quick hand speed finally gave his team an edge as he pounded his targets, temporarily paralyzing those on the receiving side.

Jack stood grinning as he pulled out a cellphone stun gun and zapped his opponents with four and a half million volts, over and over till they collapsed on the pavement and begged for mercy. He'd no intention of stopping anytime soon; a siren wailing in the distance distracted him. Some of the bikers hurried to their feet. Jack discharged the stun gun one last time before he and Mullson decide to scamper away. They weren't in any mood to explain or write a report for a minor incident, besides the chief wouldn't believe them because of their bad-boy reputation.

CHAPTER 6

With a rush of excitement and an empty road Mullson found himself doing something he'd always condemned. Along the Northern State Parkway with most of the streetlights already turned off, a black sport BMW and a Porsche 911 sped towards Long Island. Using every inch of the two lanes the cars moved back and forth, narrowly missing the concrete barrier at the center of the road, as they fought for the lead.

Jack focused ahead as the headlights of his BMW penetrated a light fog that was hovering above the road, he spotted something and wrenched the wheel right, avoiding a shattered tire in the left lane; he then swung the steering wheel to block the Porsche inching on his tail. A quick glance at his odometer showed the car was almost max, but he kept pushing.

Mullson who'd being tailing Jack swung his Porsche 911 and avoided the tire, he changed to fourth gear, then to fifth, and zoomed pass Jack. He changed down and kicked the accelerator, revving his turbo engine as he taunted Jack. By the time his car hit top speed he'd disappeared into the darkness of the night.

Jack lost control for a brief moment, but turned his car counterclockwise to match the direction it revolved — a full three hundred and sixty degree while slamming on the brakes, before coming to a standstill. He took in a whiff of smoke that filled the air; his tires burnt against the pavement, but the scent drifting in the breeze was different. Jack had a gift to sense death and knew something big was about to happen. The smell of gasoline, smoke, and fire. His eyes widened as he took another sniff. He hit start and the engine rumbled to life, he switched from manual to automatic and shoved the lever into drive.

In the Mullson's master bedroom the light was slightly dimmed, a clock radio on top of the chest indicated the time was 3:00 AM. At the center of the room Mrs. Mullson laid on a king-size bed, twisting and turning, she moaned softly as her husband slid between her legs and stroked her body. Things were getting real steamy; she jumped up out of her sleep. SIGH.

"All this sweating for nothing," she said, looking disappointed as she saw no sign of her husband.

Magarette Mullson dragged her body off the bed and drifted towards the door, tiptoed down the stairs, and headed straight to the kitchen, in the dark. She yanked the refrigerator door open and retrieved a ripe banana, much bigger than the norm. She slammed the refrigerator door shut and stood and observed the banana keenly, but had no intention of eating it. She lowered her eyes and almost tempted to open her leg, but only managed to sigh. Into the refrigerator she tossed back the banana and slammed the door.

Margarette went into the living room and turned on the television, a commercial was showing so she dashed towards her room, leaving the television on. Inside Anna's room the light was dimmed. Anna stretched across the bed with the telephone at her ear. She rushed as she heard footstep coming up the stairs, towards her.

"Tomorrow," she said, in a low tone. "Alright, I'll leave the window open. Okay, top door. Bye."

At ten past three, a silver Porsche turned into Mullson's driveway and slowly approached the garage door that had begun to open. When the door got raised high enough Mullson squeezed in beside the Expedition. He twisted the knob and opened a door that led from the garage to the living room where he entered.

The living room was illuminated by the light radiating from the television, other than the sound of the television silence filled the air. Mullson thought his family had been asleep and decided to head for the sofa; he pushed against the recliner and extended his legs. From off an end table he picked up the TV remote and skimmed through a few channels, finally stopping on one showing police and firefighters flocking the George Washington Bridge.

"The tragedy here at the George Washington Bridge is beyond our wildest imagination," the reporter's voice echoed from the television. "At least ten people are dead. Police are still investigating. The headless killer is at it again. Earlier in Hunts Point a prostitute's head came crashing onto the street from what appears to be an abandoned building."

"Too many killers," said Mullson, "not enough cops." He'd been so focused on the television he didn't even see his wife in the backdrop creeping towards him. She slid off her robe to exhibit her sexy lingerie that hugged her body, revealing in the right area, the way her man loved it.

Inside a living room, somewhere in Long Island, a sixty inch plasma television had been stuck on a channel covering the accident scene at the George Washington Bridge. They replayed footage captured by cameras on the bridge showing a Grumman Step Van speeding across the George Washington Bridge towards New Jersey. The words 'I SCREAM' was graffitied across the back of the beat-up van that cut off a tractor-trailer. The tractor-trailer, with brakes squeaking, swerved to another lane and collided with other vehicles. The overturned tractor-trailer skid along the road sweeping everything in its path.

Vehicles piled along the bridge, some bursting into flame, rocketing into the air. The 'I SCREAM' van continued ahead of the accident, nothing showed the unidentified driver. The television flicked off, leaving the room in darkness. The sounds of sex filled the air.

"You got to be kidding," said a woman, sounding disappointed.

A clap echoed and the lights came on, revealing fine Italian furniture throughout. Jack scrambled to put on his clothes while a gorgeous white chick stared at him. On the sofa she stretched out on her back with her legs opened, her clothes tossed aside on the floor. She used her hands and caressed her naked body, rubbing her legs against a velvet cover clutching the sofa. About late twenties, the woman's veins looked as if about to pop through her forehead, her mouth dropped as Jack continued to get dressed. All along she thought he'd be teasing her and waited for him to jump in.

"Okay I lied," Jack admitted. "I'm not a Jamaican."

She got even more upset at Jack for not working her pussy the way he'd bragged earlier on the phone when he called and woke her. He had her heart pounding twice as fast, and she imagined sinking her nails in his back when she climaxed-- damn. She bit her lips and clenched her fists.

"Get him Big Boy!" she yelled. A Chow-Chow came running into the living room and dashed towards Jack.

Jack grabbed his stuff and shot for the exit, as the miniature dog gave chase. He slammed the front door behind. His car rumbled to life then sped away.

Outside the Mullson's residence an early morning breeze rushing across the land cleared some of the fog hovering above the ground, smoke plummeting from a few chimneys choked life from the morning, newspapers already tossed on the lawn waited to be picked up. Inside Anna's room the light was dim. Anna was in bed tucked beneath her goose blanket. She'd finally fell asleep about an hour ago, but had begun to twist and turn, as if she sensed the presence of somebody staring at her.

Engulf with a knife hoisted above his head moved toward Anna. A quick flash as a headless Jason appeared out of thin air and punched Engulf in the face. The impact of the punch sent Engulf crashing into the dresser mirror, shattering glass in all directions.

Anna jumped out of her sleep and hurried her eyes around the room, neither Engulf nor Jason in sight, the dresser mirror stood intact, nothing seemed out of place, except for a knife on the floor she hadn't spotted. She swore she heard a shattering sound and wondered if her mind had begun to play tricks. Hesitating to go back to sleep, she forced her eyes open, but not for long, as her tired body dozed away.

On a futon shoved against the back wall of his office located in the basement, Detective Mullson had been tucked away under his robe. He leapt from his sleep and flicked a switch to brighten the room. He came down earlier to work, but took a quick nap to rid what was left of the headache from last night's episode, the sex had calmed his nerves.

The headache had become a part of Mullson's recent set of problems that constantly beleaguered him. A few days ago when he called an older friend for advice he told Mullson to go and visit a bush doctor. With all the conventional approaches he'd been told over and over, "Mr. Mullson we're sorry, there's nothing else we can do. Those medications are very powerful and should have helped to lessen your pain. Remember to take only one tablet a day, if needed."

You bet your ass they're needed, he thought, as he stooped to retrieve a bottle of Oxycontin 40 that stood on the floor next to the futon. He opened the bottle, tossed two pills in his mouth, closed his eyes then swallowed, using a finger to massage his throat as the pills slid along. Bush doctor, do I need a bush doctor?

He skimmed through months of mail that mostly ended up in the wastepaper basket. From off the computer desk he picked up a picture frame lying face down and removed a picture seemingly of himself, words scribbled across the back he read:

It's hard to say goodbye. As the time draws near,
I lived under constant pressure from within.
The pressure became so strong that I suspected
there was a psychic disturbance haunting me, which
led me to submit myself to the impulses of the
unconscious.

Love you always
Your brother Daniel

Anna turned up the lights in her room, on the floor next to the dresser her attention was eventually drawn to a knife resembling a miniature machete. That's weird, she thought, and wondered how it got there. Her parents rarely entered her room. The only person that came to mind was Daniel, an uncle who she admitted had an obsession with antique knives associated with religious quest or myths dating back thousands of years. Daniel had gotten her dad involved in a recent search for the lost knife of Satan. She knew for a fact her father wouldn't leave his toys around the house, Anna could bet on it, but she wanted to ask him anyway.

She tugged the edges of her comforter and straightened creases before placing the pillows and shams at the head of the bed. Anna recalled all those countless hours she spent with her dad on the range firing at targets. Mr. Mullson taught his whole family how to protect themselves from intruders, but, if someone broke into her room while she'd been asleep she reckoned all that training useless.

Inside the master bedroom Mrs. Mullson cuddled under a blanket, still asleep. From the master bathroom Detective Mullson exited the shower with steamy water soaking all over his body and entered the room. Across his back, legs, chest, and thighs he hurried a towel, before slipping into a blue robe. On top of a side table the phone lit up to signal and incoming call. Mullson rushed and retrieved the cordless phone from its base.

"What's really going on?" he said, walking back and forth.

"Honestly," Jack echoed from the other side.

"Go ahead," said Mullson, waiting for a reply.

"Agent Hill is willing to team up," said Jack, his voice fizzled.

"Is it that bad?" said Mullson, peeping at the clock radio on the chest. "I'm going to check a friend, why don't you meet me in the Bronx."

"After breakfast," Jack interrupted.

Mullson grinned. "Another bad night?" he teased. He dodged out of the room and descended half the flight of stairs.

"Mullson!" Magarette shouted.

"Not again," Trevor Mullson whispered beneath his breath, to himself. "I'll be back in a few," he assured his wife.

CHAPTER 7

A crow on the roof of the Mullson's house cawed occasionally and had the nosey old lady next-door wondering if they'd been up to no good. Mrs. Newton glanced at the annoying creature and could have sworn she spotted a man where the bird perched, provoking her to rip the glasses from her face and rub the lens against her dress. She'd been spying on the Mullson's residence for the past years, ever since her husband passed and she'd nothing much to do. She loves to play detective. At the side yard Mullson caught her stretching her long neck over the fence and did nothing to discourage her since information about Anna's friends can be at times vital.

A BMW came and parked on the road next to mailbox number nine hundred and ninety-nine. Jack exited the car then went and tapped on the front door. Detective Mullson pulled the door open for Jack to enter.

Mrs. Mullson woke, took a long shower, got dressed then went into the kitchen and prepared breakfast, which consisted of pancakes, scrambled eggs, and sausage.

Inside the dining room she got help from Anna to set the table, with knives, forks, spoons, plates, and cups in their assumed position.

Anna sat at the table and waited for her mother and father who'd went to the kitchen to get coffee and orange juice. On the dining table she placed the knife she found in her room. Detective Mullson came and rested a pitcher of orange juice and a pot of coffee next to the knife. "Keep your toys where they belong," said Anna.

Trevor Mullson took the knife and observed the strange encryption carved along the length of its steel frame. "That's not a part of my collection," he said.

"Why was it in my room?" said Anna.

Mullson moved toward the living room. "In your room?" he said from the living room, sounding astonished. Jack was stretched out on a recliner dozing; he jumped when he heard Mullson's voice.

After pointing Jack to the dining room Mullson went and stood staring at the rain that had begun to pound against the window. A broad smile beamed across his face, and he nodded his head with approval. How proud his mother would have felt, he thought, only if she'd been alive to share in his success. Detective Mullson loved his house he and his wife had spent the past years molding into their home. Their lifelong savings had been invested in the gorgeous two story.

At the dining table Anna, Magarette, Jack, and Trevor sat and ate the scrumptious treat.

They were halfway through the breakfast when the telephone ringing in the backdrop had Mrs. Mullson dashing towards the kitchen.

Anna slapped her head between her palms; Detective Mullson spotted her.

"What's the matter darling?" he asked.

"Nothing," said Jack, after forcing another whole pancake into his mouth.

"Not you idiot," Mullson told Jack jokingly.

"Hold up buddy," said Jack. "Thought I was the one going through the emotional breakdown." He glimpsed a familiar knife when he stretched and retrieved a pitcher containing orange juice and he poured a glass. "Holy shit!" he continued, after picking up the knife and found himself facing demons whose souls the knife had conquered.

"What's so special about it?" said Anna, to Jack.

Ask your father," Jack advised her, snapping back to reality. He turned to Mullson. "I thought you had never seen your brother?"

From the other end of the table Detective Mullson stared at Jack.

"I didn't," he said.

"Why are you so obsessed with weird UGLY machetes?" said Jack.

"Knife," Mullson corrected Jack.

Magarette came back in the dining room and whisked away a few empty plates; she headed back to the kitchen without uttering a word and tossed them on the counters and sink. Detective Mullson got up from the dining table and scurried towards his wife who had tears gushing down her cheeks. "Your daughter and I need you," she said to her husband, after sensing something bad was gonna happen by the way her right eye kept pulsating.

Only somewhat superstitious, Detective Mullson never took her words lightly. She'd saved him more than he admitted. "Sweetheart," said Mullson, to his wife.

"Mom!" Anna yelled from the dining room.

Jack stumbled in the kitchen.

"Am I interrupting?" he asked Mrs. Mullson. She jerked her head upward and gave him the evil eye. He'd been hanging with the family long enough and knew Mrs. Mullson was not in a good mood. Jack made a U-turn, but double backed and grabbed an apple from a crystal bow resting on the counter, next to the faucet. "I'll just excuse myself," he continued. Mullson watched as Jack signaled him goodbye and headed towards the front of the house. A few seconds later a door slammed and not long after a car rumbled to life.

Magarette puts the pancake syrup into the refrigerator and slammed the door. "You've spent our entire marriage with Jack chasing criminals across the globe while I sit home waiting for the past how many years!" These she said very fast without pausing.

"Come on Magarette," said Trevor. "Why are you so harsh? Seems like you forgot where we coming from."

"You don't need to remind me where we're coming from," said Magarette, grinding her teeth while peeking from beyond those squinted eyes. "What you need to do is remind yourself WHERE ARE WE GOING! Go ahead Mr. Mullson. When you escape the grip of the devil, we will be back."

On a LCD screen built-in on the door of the refrigerator Mullson glanced at the digital date: JUNE 27. "But today is my-" he said.

"Happy birthday Dad," Anna interrupted, from the living room.

"You have exactly one week," Magarette warned her husband. "Miss Anna, please get dressed… we're going to Jamaica."

Somewhere in Northern New Jersey the morning sun shined over a vast stretch of farmland growing mostly flowers and corn. Dumping grounds popped up every now and then. A Mercedes Benz crawled along the nearly deserted dirt road towards Liberty Street, where Joe and Benny had been keeping a tab on the morning. From a State Trooper car hidden among the shrubs they spotted the black car approaching. Joe, a slender thirty-nine year old fellow sat at the steering wheel. He'd been a veteran in the NJ State Police Department for the past twenty years, and now under his wing, Benny, a chubby officer who was ten years younger and sat at the front passenger seat stuffing his face with donuts.

"Here we go again," Joe pointed to Benny, with a grind flashing across his pale face.

"Joe," said Benny, flinching. "What's the matter?"

"Do you suppose that's one of them?"

"Just a little more patience Benny," the grind across Joe's face widened. "Just a little bit more."

They stared as the car got closer. The words imprinted on the tag read: MR REX. The windows tinted to the maximum allowed, fancy rims embraced each tires. The Benz had begun to make a right turn towards Liberty Street when the state trooper car emerged and blocked the road. Benny and Joe, each swinging a baton, drifted toward the Mercedes, slowly.

The driver's door swung open and a towering fellow stepped out of the Benz; he stood waiting as the two officers approached. Neither of the officers had a clue they were about to confront Mr. Rex — one of the most feared men around the Tri-state area. But this was not his domain, he'd ventured to the wrong town. In a desolated area like this the police are gods, from racial profiling to hating minorities. Not that they totally hated minorities. They don't like what they represented. *"And with them nosing around changes will follow. Heck no, not good for the community. Next thing you know they will be procreating our mighty fine gurls at Fowl Catcher Dissco — even though a few of them don't have any teeth, but they still can be work with, as long as they close 'em yawper. Yes-Siree. We might not be educated, but we're happi."*

Mr. Rex's reputation had boosted his confidence over the years, forcing him to let his guard down. Benny went to the back window and shined his flashlight; he spotted a baby secured in her seat, focusing on the light. POW! The sound of Joe's baton crushed against Mr. Rex's skull. Benny rushed over and did the same. Batons shattered against Mr. Rex's body, over and over as he screamed. He fought back, but the grip of the troopers overpowered him. They continued to hammer him even after he was stretched out on the road with his face in a puddle of his own blood, making no sound or movement. Joe looked around then pointed at the cornfield ahead. Benny nodded his head in agreement.

About an hour had passed. A Grumman 'I SCREAM' van found itself along the desolated New Jersey road leading to Liberty Street. Other than loosened soil mixed with small traces of blood there was no sign of Mr. Rex or the Benz. Joe and Benny spotted a beat-up van heading their direction, by the way the van shuffled across the narrow road Joe suspected the driver had to be drunk or blind.

The van swung left on Liberty Street, just as the patrol car emerged from the usual spot and wailed, signaling the Grumman to pull over. The van stopped on the left side of the road. The troopers suspected they were about to confront a drunkard who'd no respect for the laws. DWI, a danger to others, but they'd no intention of making an arrest. Instead they wanted to have plain old fun. Strangers venturing around these parts — not their concern; their job was to protect the few citizens scattered throughout the town like Billy Bob, the Norton family, Aunt Sally and her family, Judge Mathis, Reverend Dick Slayer, and those mighty fine girls at Fowl Catcher Disco.

Joe thundered over the intercom, "Step out of the truck, slowly. We don't want to hurt you!" Benny dragged his oversized body to the front passenger side of the Grumman van and pointed his pistol at the person who faced away.

Joe exited the trooper car; his gut feeling told him something wasn't right, maybe because he kept focusing on the 'I SCREAM' tattooed across the back of the van. He radioed for back up — the first time he actually did this. He and his partner had always handled themselves pretty well, they loved the action, writing reports. Who had time to waste? The thought alone turned their stomachs.

Joe and Benny peeked into the van. "What have we here?" said Joe, standing by the driver's side.

"What are we going do with this one?" said Benny to Joe.

"That's the ugliest nigga I ever-" Joe pointed out, before his head hit the ground while his body remained standing, all this happened in a flash.

Benny's eyes popped opened as he spotted his headless partner. The blood doubled pace through his heart. His head pounded, goose-bumps itched away on his arms and legs. He tried to move, but his feet wouldn't allow him to. He opened his mouth and only managed to force a few crackles.

Wrath stepped out of the 'I SCREAM' van, a Rastafarian hat tipped to one side of his head, a pair of sunglasses covered his eyes, and sporting the uniform of a JFK Airport Security Officer with the name-tag: JEFT. He had a machete in one hand with blood trickling from the silver-white blade.

POW! A bullet thundered toward the Frankenstein thing. Benny squeezed the trigger, again and again.

Wrath used his bare fist and punched away all the bullets reigning toward him.

Benny was out of ammo, but he continued to press the trigger. For the first time his gun had failed him. All the confidence he'd built over the few years of service began to rot away like his self esteem, like faded memories of his imagined girlfriend after losing his virginity to a

hooker he was supposed to book, all that power energiz-
ing his body after putting a smack down on Mr. Rex.

Wrath threw the machete on the ground.

Benny pulled out his flashlight and swung at Wrath.

With anger raging inside, Wrath used his hands and
ripped off Benny's head then crushed it against the patrol
car. Sirens echoing miles away had him forcing his hands
against his ears to block out the painful sound. He jumped
in his van and swirled the opposite direction, heading
back the way he came.

CHAPTER 8

T he sun penetrated the land with no signs of clouds for miles. A few apartment buildings stood on a section of sandy soil that had no room for much, other than a few spiny leafless plants with fleshy stems and branches hosting colored flowers. Further ahead where the soils bind, the ground is cracked and begging to be quench by the slightest drip, if merciful. Vehicles parked at random, with doors opened and containing purses, money, diamonds, necklaces, children toys — but no humans. Not one in sight as far as the eyes could see.

The latest version of the military fighters plane: a Black Stealth resembling an AH-64 Apache with wings of a conventional Stealth Bomber, appeared out of thin air and hovered above the apartment buildings. Mounted below its body: 30 millimeter M230 Chain Gun, AGM-114 Hellfire and Hydra 70 rocket, green bombs and missiles with expandable capability.

On the pilot's headpiece engraved the words: SILENT KILL. He poked a button and released two of the green missiles; they stopped in midair as if waiting to be commanded. His assignment was quite simple, but not easy. Foremost he must keep everything a secret. The mission was given to him because of his trustworthiness, mankind's last draw against its enemies — but whom and where are the enemies, the thought flashed across his mind.

"Enlarge!" he yelled, with a rush of confidence, shifting the war machine to the side to focus on the missiles hovering below. One of them began to break into tiny particles that seemed alive and still lingering close to the other missile, like bees in a hive. The disintegrated particles converged toward the intact missile, and underwent rapid growth, doubling in size in a matter of seconds. Silent Kill threw up a fist. "Terminate!" Upon his word the enlarged missile darted towards the earth and thundered against the ground. Dust plummeted above the spot where the future of weapons landed. Other than that there was nothing spectacular about the fireworks, for there was none. Not a single building or car seemed to be damaged.

"Silent Kill," a voice echoed over the radio, "Do you read me?" Hundreds of miles away, high voltage and off limit signs plastered on a fence surrounding a satellite dish. On the outer perimeter corpses of raccoons, Mexican gray wolves and mountain lions decayed. A Western diamondback rattlesnake sizzled after forcing its head through a hole in the fence. The land, deemed a radiation zone by federal officials, didn't seem to slow the growth of cacti and desert animals, instead, they flourished.

Hidden deep beneath the surface was a control room called Bunker X. Inside logos of the Pentagon embraced the walls, the lights radiated a greenish glow, Thermo-Hygrometer placed throughout the room monitored the icy air rushing through a side vent in the wall. State-of-the-art computers jammed on desks at the center. Soldiers sat at every computer desk. Behind them stood higher-ranking military officials, glancing at radar images. One in particular with nothing on the screen should have been showing the abandoned building Silent Kill targeted, but got knocked out. Sweat scattered over their foreheads as they waited. In the meantime as if about to eat the nails off their fingers, and kept pulling every strain of hair from their almost bald heads.

"Mission accomplished sir!" Silent Kill bellowed over the radio.

They jumped, laughed, and congratulated each other on a job well done. "No one will ever guess," said the commanding officer, a slight grin across his face.

Silent Kill stared at the abandoned building below. His eyes never drifted to the side where two men in the distance stood watching his every move. The men, about late-thirties, were mirror images of the other. Assassin #1 and Assassin #2 — the Asian twins zoomed in on the abandoned buildings; their vision appeared magnified as if some type of device were built into their eyes.

"When the time is right," said Assassin #1, "we will make a move." Assassin #2 echoed an evil laugh. A strong wind rushing across the desert swept away the abandoned buildings and vehicles, as if they were made from loose sands, spreading their particles near and far. Strangely enough the missile had caused more damage than first thought. A greener type of war had forced people to seek better ways of killing with the least amount of damage to the environment. Silent Kill felt please and jetted away. Little did he know the project sparked the interest of Engulf; anything to do with the destruction of humanity wetted the beast's appetite. Not that Engulf needed such inferior toys for his personal use; for in his heart his power equaled the gods he challenged. But chaos had a sweeter role in his quest. With his army growing larger each day he planned to unleash more wrath upon humankind, but first he must conquer the other Mullson brother.

Along the New Jersey turnpike Detective Mullson and Jack sped south. Jack drove his BMW towards a shoulder then cut ahead of other vehicles. Mullson followed in his 911 Carerra. Both men had sirens on the dash of their cars, and neither was wailing. They drove and drove, switching lanes like maniacs to avoid the slowing of traffic; a jam further ahead had a trickling effect. Some of the more heated motorists honked their horns at the two impatient bastards. Jack and Mullson had no time to retaliate as they would; they were summoned to help with a case in New Jersey and they hurried to get to Liberty Street. Agent Hill buzzed them more than once, the fact that he despised their reputation and was willing to join the team was extremely important — and they knew it.

They took a sharp right and exited to a rocky road where they drove until they spotted Liberty Street that had been blocked off by State Troopers. Canine dogs and their masters had been rushing through rows of corns and flowers in nearby fields. The dogs sensed something ahead, where tracks of a vehicle plunging over rows of corn had left a dent, but their handlers turned them away, as if preventing the uncovering of the town's secrets. The troopers did their best to hide all the evidence pointing toward the middle of the field.

This department in particular had a lot to hide. After the FBI had targeted them for racial profiling a few years back many of the troopers sought revenge. Joe had taught them how to eliminate the enemies without leaving a trace, so it was personal to lose one of their brightest stars. Even more disrespectful was for outsiders to fringe upon their privacy, their way of living, and all the things they fought to preserve over the years. The Feds weren't welcome and now they sent for those two arrogant bastards from New York, with all 'em fancy cars — what the hell is this world coming to — all sort of things raced through the troopers' minds, and a gleam of suspicion flashed across their faces.

At the junction Agent Hill and Agent McKoy inspected a pool of blood. Detective Mullson and Jack parked their cars, and walked toward several troopers who stared at them up and down, mostly focusing on Mullson. Two troopers built like gladiators and resembling drill sergeants meeting privates for the first time, advanced toward their prey. One stood before Mullson with a rather wicked grin, the other before Jack, denying them entry.

Jack and Mullson held their ground.

"Step aside bitches," Jack lashed out at the two men. "Don't you recognize trouble?" he pointed at Mullson. "By the way, today is his birthday." The two troopers retreated after Agent Hill and Agent McKoy rushed over to Jack and Mullson.

"Welcome gentlemen," said Hill. He looked Mullson in the face. "Heard you're a bad ass— nothing personal, I don't give a damn-" He pointed at McKoy, "This is my partner Agent McKoy."

She shoved her hand forward.

"Hi, nice meeting you Detective Mullson," she said. Detective Mullson gripped her hand gently, and almost got the life squeezed out of his.

"Nice meeting you too Agent McKoy," he said. A ringtone echoed from his cellular phone. He whisked it to his ear, "Hello, hello, hello!" Mullson pressed the END button after listening to the silence from the other side for more than a minute. As he was about to toss the phone back in the case clenching to his belt it sang again.

"You have until midnight," said a distorted voice over the phone.

"Who's this?" said Mullson, his bushy brows squinted out of control. CLONK! The telephone slammed in his ear had his mind racing as fast as the blood gushing through his veins. He seemed dumbstruck and tried to mask his emotion as Jack, Agent Hill, and Agent McKoy stood waiting for him to say something. Jack sensed something was wrong.

"What's that about?" he asked Mullson.

"I don't know," said Mullson. "Feels like I'm constantly being watched." He thought about what he'd asked Father Andrew earlier, on the plane "don't tell me people who died in the line of duty comes back to haunt us." Maybe, Father Andrew's voice echoed in his head.

"What's the matter pal?" said Jack, tapping on Mullson's shoulder.

Mullson glanced at his watch as the sun sneaked behind a cloud; the time read 11:45. Driven by instinct he went and surveyed the spot where Mr. Rex got disciplined, and found a large platinum necklace partially buried in the dirt. Mullson handed Agent Hill the necklace. "It belongs to Mr. Rex," he said.

Jack stared at the fresh cover of dirt hiding the blood beneath. "Mr. Rex as in Rexan?" he said, to Mullson.

"His wife contacted the FBI and reported him and the child missing," said Agent McKoy.

"What makes you so sure Detective Mullson?" said Agent Hill, observing the pendant that spotted the word MR. REX surrounded by diamonds. He moved towards several troopers who had been isolating themselves, and stood at the spot where Benny and Joe used to hide in their patrol car. These men had their eyes on every movement, and already planned not to cooperate with any outsiders willingly.

Jack glanced at his wrist and thought his watch had to be broken, for 12:30 p.m. had totally caught him off guard.

Agent McKoy made note of the different personalities around her, all along she'd suspected the troopers were not telling them the whole story. What happened to the camera mounted on the dash? The department is cutting back on budget is not an excuse why the equipment malfunctioned. She searched her cranium to put the puzzle together. Maybe they're just protecting their asses. She led on to agree with their story. A killer on the loose was her major concern.

All along Mullson thought about the strange call; he sneaked a peek at the time, and had begun to wonder if his wife and daughter were okay, earlier when he buzzed them he'd no luck.

"Let's go," he told Jack, already scurrying towards his car.

"May I ask where?" Agent McKoy blunted, to Mullson. He finally told her he'd met a couple on the plane that could shed some light about one of the victims at JFK. McKoy seemed interested and signaled her partner to hurry along. A serial killer was on the loose and God forbid the public get ahold of the information not available to them as yet. With time against them they needed to act fast. And they did just that. Jack and Mullson revved their engines and had their tires rocketing stones and dirt in the opposite direction, before speeding away. Agent McKoy and Agent Hill jumped in their FBI sedan and followed.

The troopers sighed in relieved when the outsiders began to retreat. Knowing the FBI would be back they gathered and began to chitchat, hoping to straighten any deviation in their stories and to seek revenge for their fallen comrades. First they must ask Reverend Dick Slayer to pray for their souls. Next they planned to question those mighty fine girls at Fowl Catcher Disco; if any stranger passed through they were usually the first to know.

It was later in the day when Mullson and his team arrived at a single family house surrounded by freshly cut lawn and colorful flowers in a small New Jersey town closer to New York. At the front of the house red bricks layered while the side and back were covered with hardiplank. A bird feeder hanging above a small garden attracted mostly chickadees, titmice, and finches. Squirrels chased each other among a clutter of trees further at the side yard, where a yellow-bellied sapsucker paused as Mullson, Jack, Agent Hill and McKoy marched towards the front door.

Mullson tapped against the doorbell, repeatedly, and a buzzing sound echoed from the midst of the house. They stood waiting, but nobody came out. Detective Mullson thought about his wife and daughter the whole morning, an appointment he had with Father Johnson who supposedly lived somewhere in Upstate New York, and an early retirement to toss at his department that expected so much from him, especially with the recent series of headless killings. He'd not yet told Jack about his plan to retire. SIGH.

Ever since Mullson got back from Africa Jack sensed their friendship was coming to an end. He enjoyed every bit of their companionship, yet the fact Mullson had been drawing closer to two particular priests rattled his nerves. Being a human has its advantage, but Jack would rather be his old self where he's used to commanding with an iron fist; having his desires flamed by a raging fire, literally, and where the screaming of souls sounded like sweet music to his ears. He respected Mullson for not questioning his religious beliefs. From the day of his creation Jack opposed God's plan for mankind, but that he must keep to himself since he didn't wants to disturb all them religious folks hanging around.

Agent McKoy and Agent Hill pulled their guns then headed to the back of the house, leaving Mullson and Jack at the front, still waiting for an answer. "But you just spoke to them," Jack reminded Mullson. "Let's go inside to see what's wrong."

"We have no warrant," Mullson warned Jack, like he expected it would make a difference. Before he finished the conversation Jack had already raised his foot and smashed it against the door, collapsing the outer wooden door as well as an inner one.

"I have a warrantee on my boots," Jack bragged to Mullson — who stood staring at both doors on the floor and was too shocked to comprehend the power of Jack's leg. At the backyard Agent McKoy had already kicked-in the solid door from off the frame. Agent Hill glanced at the door on the ground, then at McKoy. "Oh my God," he said, running a hand through the hair on his head.

"Move it sir!" said Agent McKoy, storming into the house and flashing her pistol from side-to-side. Her partner followed and they scanned every inch of the family room which contained a sectional and a small television resting on a wall unit. Most notable was the icy air rushing from the AC that froze the room. The first thing that flashed across McKoy's mind — "Iceman" experiments with disguising the time of death of his victims by freezing their corpses. Inside the living room, Jack and Mullson entered with their weapons pointing and spotted what appeared to be a man and a woman sitting in a loveseat, facing away. A collection of antique knives inside a glass case was shoved against the wall, perpendicular to the loveseat. Mullson couldn't help but notice a rack that had one knife missing. Picture of the Jefts family embraced the wall, wherever space was available for the large frames.

The old couple didn't move a bone as Jack teased loudly, "How do we say hello in sign language?"

"Hello," McKoy voiced rumbled from the back of the house, "anyone home?"

Still the couple did not move. Mullson shuffled to the other side of the loveseat and recognized the pair as the Jeft couple he'd met on the plane a few days ago. Luckily Mrs. Jeft had slipped him an old business card, that's where he got the address Conrad Jeft used awhile back for a PI firm he'd started, but the company didn't material-ize— Mullson had a friend run some background checks.

"Anyone home," said Agent Hill, in the backdrop.

"In the living room!" said Jack, signaling Agent Hill and McKoy, who tumbled in with their weapon still drawn.

Mullson returned his gun to the holster, and stared at the couple. There was something odd about the way they sat with their eyes wide open and their bodies stiff and lifeless like zombies. Their skin had begun to turn slightly purple. Mrs. Jeft's once rosy cheeks looked paled. "What happened?" said Agent McKoy, shoving the .45 in her holster.

"Something is not right," said Jack, his gun pointed to the floor as he shuffled closer to Mullson.

"Everything seems fine to me," Agent Hill echoed, just to oppose Jack. To prove his point he passed Mullson and went and tapped the Jefts on their shoulders, gently. He jumped as Mr. and Mrs. Jeft's heads separated from their bodies and hit the floor with a thud.

CHAPTER 9

The sun took a quick break behind a stretch of clouds, but that didn't make a difference to the campers below who had the luxury of dense vegetation that offered protection from the deadly rays. Rapid busts from a M16A2 that echoed from the midst of the woods had soldiers dodging behind trees, some tucking away in foxholes. M60 machine guns rumbled to life, followed by the booming of grenades. A thunderous squeal that erupted long after a plane left a nearby airbase had them scanning the sky. Only a trail of smoke scattered by the wind was visible. It was a raucous scene simulating a war as troops engaged in a day of training at one of the New Jersey facilities.

On the outskirts of the camp, further away from the training area, Wrath had been crunching among some shrubs, a sniper rifle on the ground laid arms length away. Wearing battle uniforms he blended in perfectly with the other soldiers he spotted. Still peeping through the binoculars he focused on a small wooden cabin concealed by twigs, a splash of green and brown paint gave it a sense of naturalness. A jeep was parked approximately fifty feet away from the cabin, the driver kept checking his timepiece as he stood waiting.

Several soldiers with live rounds in their magazines stood guarding the perimeter.

Two priests, one with a textbook tucked away under his arm, exited the cabin. Two soldiers escorted them towards the jeep; the driver hopped in and picked up a walkie-talkie. Inside the cabin, sunlight penetrating through leaves and branches barely lit the ten-by-ten space that had a reek of tobacco and kerosene cluttering the air. A lantern hung from a post supporting the roof, a walkie-talkie and an opened attaché case containing money rested on a small table located at the center, two cots were folded and placed in one corner opposite the entrance, a M203 leaned against one of the cots.

A bulky white fellow in his early fifties eyed the money and with a wicked grin he snatched a pile. Years of combat had left no dent on one of the toughest marines on the planet. Captain Austin prided himself with producing some of the finest men money cannot buy. Well, the church had offered him a generous donation for finding and returning an old text book they'd been seeking. He'd begun to wonder what made them so sure about that particular book, Dark Secrets. Only if he could read the ancient script handwritten with ink across every other page.

"The root of all evil," he said, sniffing the money. "Yet smells so good."

"Sir," a male voice crackled over the walkie-talkie as the sounds of a vehicle rumbled to life. "It's time."

Austin advanced toward the door; he paused and listened as two shots rang out in the backdrop. To him they sounded more like live rounds. His instinct told him something was wrong, and he followed it and peeped through a small hole. He blinked twice and spotted a M203 aiming at his niche.

The jeep stood idling after its driver had bullets explode in each of his eyes. The soldiers who were guarding the priests never got a chance to react as their bodies got riddled, the priests scrambled away, but it was too late. They'd come to protect the future of humankind, to prevent the book from evil, all hopes faded as their life departed, and the old textbook lying in a puddle of blood read: Dark Secrets.

With his size-thirteen boot braced against Wrath's back restraining him to the ground, Engulf squeezed the trigger of a M203 grenade launcher he blasted without mercy. He stood tall in a black combat uniform, the one he chose for his gang that they embraced with pride. Engulf had rallied the army of darkness and wanted

Wrath to be second in command; this test was supposed to prove his commitment.

"Afraid to kill, are we?" he jeered Wrath who fought hopelessly to be set free. Engulf pointed the M203 at the cabin and watched as it exploded, after pressing his index against the trigger of the grenade launcher.

Soldiers returned fire. Three AH-64 Apache Helicopters came and hovered above the camp, they fired at the man in the black suit.

Engulf grabbed the sniper rifle and darted into some bushes for coverage; Wrath followed closely. The three Apaches searched the perimeter for intruders who had demolished their pride, the ranks they'd fought so long to protect, and their reputation as the elite of the military. The enemies needed to be defeated and at all means they planned to annihilate them, as soon as they figured where they lurked. The two officers aboard Apache #1 scanned from left to right, their hearts raced as they fired at movement they thought was unusual. What resembled a giant bullet punctured the window and went straight through the ears of the pilot, whose death was greeted without the slightest warning. Apache #1 swerved out of control and tumbled from the sky. A crashing boom followed after it hit a tree and burst into flames, shattering into pieces. From the two remaining helicopters, bullets reigning from 30-millimeter M230 Chain Gun under the aircraft's forward fuselage treaded everything in their path.

The Black Stealth appeared out of thin air, prowling ahead, and came towards the two Apaches that suddenly shift backward, slowly, with the AGM-114 Hellfire and Hydra 70 rocket mounted on stub-wing pylons armed and aimed at the stealth. The officers abroad the Apaches sweated profusely as the strange war-machines edged away at their position.

For what and who they faced had neither heart nor compassion, they knew nothing about: love, order, peace, prosperity. Their souls hardened by the will to serve their master who lurked among humankind, blending in with civilizations, and preying upon any weakness to further undermine the system. Silent Kill wouldn't harm them, at least, not intentionally.

Pilots aboard the Apaches had never confronted anything like the Black Stealth whose defensive system reacted according to what they tossed at it — the hellfire and hydra 70 rockets did not penetrate the recently discovered alloyed Indestructium enclosing the Stealth framework. There was speculation about the military using alien technology salvaged during a crash landing somewhere in Arizona to construct a super plane, but the government denied such an allegation and instead credited the American chemist and artist Masta Recka for his insightful thoughts that led to the creation of Indestructium.

The two Apaches tried with all their might, and now they waited for the final judgment, after the opponent had proven to be quicker and swifter. The Black Stealth rocketed two missiles towards the choppers — they swung in all directions, making a series of sharp turns, but the missiles kept taunting them, at times adjusting speed to remain thirty feet away from the targets.

Without parachutes on, and the fact there were stones and other blunt objects piled hundreds of feet below, soldiers aboard the Apaches jumped out when they spotted a gush of smoke as the missiles made the final move. Plummeting from the sky the choppers' blades ripped away branches from the tops of trees. Upon hitting the ground they continued to plowed dirt, stones, shrubs and trees, human remains. All this happened in a chaotic order until finally, BOOM, the earth shook as fragments of metals and other objects got hurled in all directions, fire and smoke choked the atmosphere with toxic fumes rocketing above the surface. The missiles paused in midair and returned to their original position under the Stealth, without exploding.

Wrath dodged behind trees, one after the other as the Stealth shattered them with small precision rockets about the size of a giant bullet damaging only the intended target. Wrath managed to dig himself from a pile of rubble and limped further into the woods where he escaped.

Inside the Stealth, Assassins #1 and #2 were in total control. Silent Kill was not onboard. There were splatters of blood on the seats and windows.

The two Assassins and Engulf communicated using their telepathic power. "Sir, sir!" Assassin #2 echoed in Engulf's head. "I'm okay," Engulf assured them. "What about the others?" Assassin #2 continued.

"Congratulations guys," said Engulf. "I need you to." "Go ahead sir," Assassin #2 encouraged Engulf, after waiting for a few seconds. "Get rid of Trevor Mullson," Engulf mind infuriated, "And his family tree." "Thought he was useless?" Assassin #1's mind blurted.

"Not according to the prophecy," Engulf warned.

"What about your father?" Assassin #1's mind raced. "That traitor," Engulf reminded them. "Just do as I said."

The Stealth resting in the skyline above the woodland finally zoomed into the clouds. Engulf headed further into the woods.

Inside Bunker X, Military officials continued to monitor the main radar control unit, long after the three dots they were tracking disappeared from the screen.

The captain ran his hand across his head and sighed. "Sir," he said to the Commander. "I am deeply sorry."

"We worked so hard," said the Commander, walking in circle. His face got redder as the clock ticked away. "Yet this is the reward. Gentleman. What am I going to tell the President of the United States?"

"It's hard to believe Silent Kill betrayed us," the Captain pointed out to the Commander who seemed dazed.

Outside the Jeft's house, Crime Scene Unit blocked off the perimeter; neighbors drawn by flashing lights came and inquired about what had happened. Inside, Mullson and his comrades scanned every inch of the house, hoping to find some clues, anything that will give them a bit of hope to stop the senseless killing. The FBI put out a field alert for a possible serial killer haunting the Tri-state area. With no lead, and frustration pounding, all Mullson and his team could do was wait for a break. Killers always make mistakes, and they prayed for sooner than later.

Mullson punched a few keys on his cell phone and listened to the dial tones.

Inside a room where the lights had been dimmed, a person facing away and wearing a pair of latex gloves plunged a pair of scissors into a human stomach. The phone rang. "I'm in the middle of a feast," a man whispered, after retrieving the phone he forced against his shoulder and ear.

"This is not the time to fool around," Detective Mullson voice echoed.

"All work and no play makes Mullson a dull boy," the man continued while using one hand to yank out the heart as he dissected a body. He turned and almost fell; the clumsy scientist ripped open a bag and removed Jeft's head. "The cause of death, headless. Weapon, still unknown."

"Make room for the parents," said Mullson, his voice sounding distressed.

"Kidding. Are you?" said the scientist, with a grin across his face. "Someone called, mentioned some sort of alpha cobra."

"Please hang up or dial again," a computerized voice interrupted.

"Hello," the Scientist shouted into the phone, and realized Mullson had hung up.

Detective Mullson, Jack, Agent Hill and McKoy rushed out of the Jeft house and headed towards their cars. The crime scene was still under investigation and a senior officer from New Jersey PD was left in charge. Agent Hill mumbled something to him then tailed Mullson and Jack who had almost reached their rides. "Where are we going?" Hill asked Mullson who jumped into his Porsche and cranked the engine without saying a word. The paleness in Mullson's usually intense eyes and the way his body trembled as if panic was rushing through his veins had Agent Hill and McKoy follow without further question. They sped along a dirt road, until further ahead they spotted a group of men wearing black combat uniforms. As they got closer they realized the men were armed with futuristic weapons, standing by three Jeeps parked at the side of the dirt trail, looking out.

The detectives got more than edgy when they couldn't identify the black uniform worn by the suspicious group; the only affiliations came to their minds — the Black Panther movement that died years back, maybe a private security firm, a swat team nobody recalled deploying.

With a compact Rocket Launcher placed on one shoulder, a man hurried towards the center of the road and aimed.

Mullson, who was on his way to check Captain Austin, swung the steering; his car skidded, avoiding the rocket that rumbled ahead. The heat from the ruckus scorched his body; with a narrow escape he continued to slam on the accelerator, closing the gap while keeping his head low as bullets whined by.

Jack spotted the explosion and ran his BMW into a bump that sent his car flipping through the air. The BMW landed on its four wheels as it left the explosion behind. Jack pressed his foot against the pedal and continued forward. The FBI sedan stopped short of the explosion.

Mullson and Jack accelerated toward the three Jeeps. The gangbanger fired at them with deadly intent.

Jack and Mullson pulled out their Glocks 34 and returned fire, but all in vain. They suddenly stopped their cars and both picked up a bushmaster from a hidden component below their passenger seats. In a matter of seconds the men were overpowered, after Mullson and Jack pressed their fingers against the trigger, and emptied their thirty round clips. Jack and Mullson, brandishing Remington ACR Assault Rifles, stood over the group of dead men. Agent Hill and McKoy joined them.

"Was all this killing necessary?" said Agent Hill, with a grin across his face. He felt relieved and checked his clothes for any sign of bullet holes.

By the time Mullson and his team got to the camp, it was only to find the place torched, bloody, body parts scattered; they searched the surrounding area over and over, yet no survivors turned up.

"It's too late!" said Detective Mullson, spinning in a circle as he grasped his head.

They began to put away their weapons, but Jack was not so convinced. He sniffed his way to the burned down rubble where the cabin once stood and emptied a round from his bushmaster.

"Come out with your hands up!" he shouted. Agent Hill glanced at him.

"Is he always this crazy?" he asked Mullson.

Mullson turned to face Hill who hurriedly wiped the grin off his face. "Not Jack," said Mullson.

Nobody knew much about Jack — the man who always seemed to be in the right place for the right kill. He could sense his enemies from miles away, as if he knew their thoughts, families, friends, finances. Jack loves chaos and over the years dragged his partner into his circle. Well, he had no choice but to keep Mullson closer than his enemies, after his psychic ability failed to penetrate Mullson's cranium.

"Final warning!" Jack bellowed.

"Okay," a man voice erupted from the rubbles. "Don't shoot!"

Agent McKoy ran over and stood next to Jack, she found his instinct more than extraordinary, and began to like him even more, a lot more. His bad-boy approach had her weak in the knees. Damn, she admitted to herself.

They pointed weapons at the rubble that ruffled as a trap door on the floor of the destroyed cabin shoved open. A man wearing a raggedy battle uniform emerged.

"Captain Austin!" said Detective Mullson, running over to greet him.

"Mullson!" said Captain Austin, as they shook hands.

Mullson signaled the rest of his team to join him. "What is going on?" he asked Austin. Captain Austin glanced at Jack.

"Your buddy's nose is sharper than a bloodhound," he told Mullson.

"Think this is an inside job?" Mullson asked Austin, avoiding the Jack critique.

"My Seals would never betray me," Captain Austin blurted.

"Are you saying they'd nothing to do with this?" said Mullson, using a hand to wipe away the sweat gathered on his forehead. He'd already made up his mind, from the look of things it seemed to be an outside job, but he just wanted an opinion.

Captain Austin gazed into Mullson's piercing eyes, before turning away and scanning the area. The sight of his men lying around had his heart double paced as the hot blood rushed throughout his veins; only if he could catch those bastards who tormented his soul. He clenched his fist and bit down on his lip. Austin will not stop till he gets those perpetrators, he promised himself.

"You were my very best soldier," he said to Mullson. He pointed towards bodies scattered on the ground. "As well as the rest of these guys."

All sorts of crazy ideas had begun to plague Agent McKoy mind: first she'd try to figure out possible suspects, organization, only if Jack and Mullson had left one of those fellows alive. Well, a little too dicey she agreed. "Who's bold enough to risk going to war with the Navy Seals?" she asked.

"Unless there's something more important than life the good captain is not telling us about," said Agent Hill, he'd been holding his tongue for way too long now.

Jack stared into the woods in the direction Wrath and Engulf had disappeared. For some strange reason he figured the war had begun and there was not much humankind could do to stop the domination of the fallen, not much he could do to save his long lost son whose ego now threatened the family order.

CHAPTER 10

Hidden among a patch of overgrown shrubs, a large one-story warehouse sat on the outskirt of a small town — its zinc roof corroded, cracks in the walls resembling dendrites could be spotted all over, doorposts had begun to rot away, and windows that were not shattered had dust plastered all over. A path carved through nearby woods leading to the back of the building was filled with boot marks, freshly printed.

Inside a large open room was lit by the evening sun seeping through broken windows, the stench of musk and grease filled the air. Tables and chairs were bundled at the center of the room where Engulf stood rushing through and old textbook.

Assassin #1 and Assassin #2 stood facing each other; they appeared to be in a discussion.

Engulf flipped through the book, faster and faster until he reached the end. He snatched the book off the table and slammed it against the floor. The cover of the book revealed the title: DARK SECRETS. He tossed a clenching fist in the air followed by a clean kick that sent the book hurling to the far side of the room.

It was early in the evening when Mullson and his team reached Father Johnson's Church, located in a small suburban New York town. As the helicopter began its descent, Mullson stared out the window and noticed the church appeared to be an exact replica of the one in the Bronx where he thought Father Andrew still resided, except this one was about half the size. The land surrounded by dense vegetations was much larger, only a small section had been cleared for the building and yard space.

Father Johnson accompanied by two priests exited the church then went and stood at the front after they heard the sound of a helicopter rattling above. Debris twirled about as the chopper landed at an opened area to the side. They lifted their hands before their faces and peeked as Mullson, Jack, Hill and McKoy jumped out of the helicopter and came towards them. Jack stopped and waited at a good distance while his comrades rushed towards the three priests. The helicopter ascended and returned in the direction it came.

Father Johnson used his staff and hurried toward Detective Mullson who was running ahead of his team. "Where is it?" he asked, extending his hand towards Mullson as if he expected something.

"Home," said Mullson to Father Johnson. "Found it in my daughter's room."

A strange look lashed across Father Johnson's face, his rugged brow flinched, and his eyes widened. The staff he gripped in one hand almost crumpled from the burden of his body, but he managed to shift the weight to his stronger leg.

"Where is your daughter?" he asked Mullson, a sound of panic flushed his voice.

"She is staying with her Grandmother," Mullson replied, after a slight hesitation.

They walked towards the church, Mullson signaled Jack to follow.

"Where?" Father Johnson demanded. His hair rose at the back of his neck as he glanced at Jack who stood at the outer perimeter.

In Montego Bay, Jamaica, a cool evening breeze sweeping across the airport had old folks grabbing their hats, young girls gripping their dresses as they got hurled about exposing their underwear, garbage got blown around, the aroma of food followed the wind. Seagulls extended their wings and drifted above the water pounding against cliffs — in some areas rushing deep inland until the waves broke free.

Air Jamaica had circled the sky several times; the pilot hoped for the burst of wind that dispersed the clouds to calm. After a few minutes everything was back to normal. The plane aligned with the runway ahead, slowly descended, until its wheels pounded against the pavement.

Inside the plane Mrs. Mullson and Anna sat next to each other; they clinched to their seat as the plane rocketed down the runway before coming to a halt. After the plane was secured at the gate people hurried to exit, almost running along the passageway as they raced to customs.

Outside, a taxi pulled up across from where Mrs. Mullson and Anna stood waiting by their luggage. Mrs. Mullson had recognized the tall and rugged fellow sitting at the steering wheel and decided it was okay to charter him. Before she could finish telling her location, the fellow popped the trunk open and shoved the three suitcases and a carryon in, before forcing it shut. He opened the rear passenger door and waited for Mrs. Mullson and Anna to sit before he closed it.

The taxi sped along a windy stretch of road. Anna's eyes widened as she stared at emerald green and bluish water splashing against white sand beaches, clusters of colorful flowers scattered among woodlands and meadows, mountains and valleys, several mansions on top of hills overlooking the bay, and hotels and villas along the beaches. The taxi driver glanced at his rearview mirror to make sure his passengers were comfortable.

"My name is Mr. Busy," he said in a heavy Jamaican accent. "Welcome to Jamaica beautiful ladies. This is God's paradise."

The Mullsons did not say much as their minds raced all over. Trevor Mullson was left behind to fend for himself in America. Anna did not like what was happening to her father and mother. She prayed for things to be better between the two. Both hardheaded parents of hers drove her nuts over their pettiness. High on the hillside Anna spotted a Georgian mansion with a stone base and a plastered upper story, with a panoramic view over the coast.

"That's a beautiful house," she said, pointing.

"Woman bite yu ten finga," said Mr. Busy, sounding panicky. "Yu point on duppy house! Yu never hear 'bout the White Witch of Rose Hall?"

Anna, Mrs. Mullson, and Mr. Busy walk towards the entrance of Rose Hall; two caretakers greeted and invited them in. Built in the 1770s, Rose Hall was restored in the 1960s to its former splendor, with mahogany floors, interior windows and doorways, paneling and wooden ceilings. Downstairs had a bar and a restaurant. The place had been converted to a museum for tourists who were curious about where Annie Palmer ate, slept and haunted. Inside, the trio followed the two caretakers as they headed towards the master bedroom located on the other side of the house.

Goosebumps rose at the back of Magarette Mullson's neck as the childhood thought of Annie Palmer rushed through her mind, after she managed to stop thinking about Trevor for a brief moment. She'd begun to wonder if the trip was necessary, since she felt the same raging motion eating away at her conscience.

"Please don't touch anything," one of the caretakers warned, with a strong Jamaican accent.

"Whatever you do don't say her name," the other caretaker advised, widening her eyes as the words echoed.

They finally entered the master bedroom where the lights shone dim. The caretakers wasted no time as they pointed out spots of blood on the walls and floors they believed to have survived hundreds of years — a never ending reminder of the victims of Annie Palmer whose souls continued to roam the room. All attempts to disintegrate the blood failed.

A rush of cold air swept across Anna's face as she focused on a portrait of the late Annie Palmer. She somehow sensed the presence of someone watching them, but with all the stories tossing around she let it slide. "Goodbye Annie Palmer," she whispered.

The lights flickered for seconds at a time, leaving the room dark as an eclipse at midnight. Creepy-crawlers scattered throughout, a foul smell cluttered the air, insects echoed in the backdrop. Whatever was happening had to be unusual, but the ghost hunters failed to detect any sort of paranormal activities when invited awhile back. The eerie sounds of ghostly noises penetrated the darkness, as if it had turned to midnight. Anna screamed when she spotted the portrait of the beautiful Annie Palmer who was transformed into a picture of an evil looking old lady with what appeared to be live centipedes dangling out of her mouth. By the time the light settled, everything appeared normal — no centipedes or old lady to disturb the portrait, no creepy-crawlers. Everything, except for a large green lizard with half of a centipede stuck in its mouth, the other half fought to set free as it griped into the side of the lizard that became paralyzed. Everybody rushed to get out of the room. Mrs. Mullson and Anna swore not to return, both caretakers planned to quit, Mr. Busy got even more scared of the place.

The evening sun had begun to fade over Long Island, New York. A taxi screeched to a halt before the Mullson's residency, blocking off Anna's Expedition parked in the driveway. At the back of the car both doors swung open, three men who appear to be in their early twenties exited and headed towards Mullson's front door, each carrying a suitcase.

Johnny P, black, tallest of the three, platinum crown covering his teeth, pressed the doorbell. "Guess we have to use the top door," he turned and told his two friends.

Pain Killer, a short Latino fellow, had a grin rushing across his face. "That's what I'm talking about," he said, his eyes widened with excitement. "Taking the initiative dude... yow Murf!"

The white dude seemed uneasy about the whole ordeal. "Yes Pain Killer," he stuttered, "T-t-talking to me?"

"Yes you mother-sucker," said Pain Killer, to Murf.

"I just don't like the top door," said Murf, looking up at a second floor window.

"I just don't like the top door..." Pain Killer jeered.

"Let's go," Johnny P demanded.

"They're in Jamaica," said Pain Killer. "We could chill for awhile."

The three men scampered to the side of the house and stood below Anna's room window. From out of his suitcase Pain Killer pulled out a crossbow and a ninja grappling hook attached to a rope; he fired it at an eighty degree angle and watched it arch over the roof. The hooks unfolded and penetrated the target. Pain Killer yanked on the rope several times, then climbed to the top and slid Anna's window open, to him this appeared natural. With a dull pain digging into their arms, Murf and Johnny P hauled their body to the top, one after the other, and were more than exhausted as they hurled their carcasses to the floor, while Pain Killer did a few push-ups.

Little did they know the next-door neighbor had being nosing around. Nothing escaped Mrs. Newton who stretched her neck to peep from her window and spotted the three culprits breaking into the Mullson's home. She'd been playing detective for quite sometime now, but today she finally had some luck to put her skills to the test; no more practicing with her nine cats and the countless plants she spoke to daily. With the warm blood rushing through her veins, Mrs. Newton pumped her arms and widened her stride as she dashed for the telephone at the other side of the room. She snatched the phone from the base, stuck a finger in the nine-slot and rotated the dial clockwise, followed by one, twice.

Father Johnson came towards the pulpit and stared at the high ceiling.

"The time has come for the church to repay," he warned.

Jack and Agent Hill seemed somewhat disturbed as they listened. "What exactly are we talking about Father André?" a suspicious Jack asked.

"That's not Father Andrew," Mullson corrected him. Father Johnson glanced at Jack and somehow thought this man cannot be trusted, but grabbed a hold of himself for being too judgmental.

"Excuse my manners," he said. "My name is Father Johnson."

Agent McKoy had being thinking where she came across the name before.

"Heard about you in one of my religion classes," she said to Father Johnson, after figuring it out. "Demonic twins." A broad smile ripped across Father Johnson's face.

"I can assure you things were blown out of proportion," he said to McKoy. He turned and headed to the far end of the room. "My fate awaits me," Father Johnson continued. "The falling of the sun will mark my reunion with Father Andrew."

"Where is Father Andrew?" said Detective Mullson.

"Follow me please," Father Johnson blurted.

He took them to a secret passageway leading to an underground tunnel. Upon entering the tunnel Father Johnson struck a match and lit an old lantern dangling from the ceiling; he used the lantern to fight his way through the dark and musky tunnel.

Detective Mullson scanned every inches of the tunnel and wondered what laid ahead; thoughts of Father Andrew, Anna and Magarette Mullson raced through his mind, these images got stronger as he focused ahead.

For some strange reason Jack had already figured where they were going, and what will happen, almost like a déjà vu, but stronger. What he'd been experiencing wasn't only a compelling sense of familiarity or eeriness. After trying to dampen his fear for the church his spirit had found new meaning — good must coincide with evil in order for prosperity to reign. In his eyes evilness always added the right spark to life, making us nervous, sad, happy, greedy.

Father Johnson braced against a section of the tunnel wall that opened like a door, revealing a small room filled with mice and roaches scattering into holes as the light beamed inside, cobwebs packed with spiders dangled from all corners of the room. Upon entering the room Father Johnson secured the lantern on a hook extending from the middle of the ceiling. Detective Mullson, Jack, Agent Hill, Agent McKoy, and the two priests crammed into the room.

On the wall Father Johnson tapped one of several protruding bricks and the door slammed shut.

"I am superstitious about men with superior hearing," he blurted.

"That should explain why we're down here," said Agent McKoy, glancing at Father Johnson from the corner of an eye. The room reeking of rodents and insects turned her stomach.

"You're all liable for the conversation in this room," said Father Johnson, as he swung around and faced Agent McKoy.

"I'm confused about the sun falling from the sky," said Detective Mullson, to Father Johnson. "You don't mind rephrasing?"

Father Johnson took a deep breath and exhaled. "God must have been angry at the church," he said.

"Got to be a reason," said Agent McKoy, to Father Johnson, trying to prolong the conversation.

The whole time had passed without a word from Hill or Jack, both men had learned to respect the church, but neither cared much about Father Johnson blabbing his mouth. They were seeking answers to help solve the murder mystery at hand. Mullson was quite confident he brought them to the right place.

"He's angry at mankind for uniting goodness with evil," said Father Johnson. "Engulf, the Angel of Confusion…" he turned and spotted their doubtful faces. "This is not making any sense," he continued.

"Who is this Engulf person?" said Agent McKoy, glancing at Mullson.

"The last son of Satan," said Mullson. "According to legend he's more powerful and conniving than his father."

Jack heard something that had the hot blood rushing through his body double pace. "Says who?" he asked Mullson, sounding somewhat defensive.

"Very good my son," Father Johnson nodding at Mullson, "couldn't have said it better."

"Those were Father Andrew's words," Mullson acknowledged.

"You NYPD are not so bad after all," Agent McKoy told Mullson.

"You're not buying that nonsense," said Agent Hill, to McKoy. "ARE YOU?"

"I am not buying the part where the son beat up the father," said Jack to Hill, anger raging in his voice. "Where I'm from that son would eat his balls. BY FORCE!" his voiced pierced the room and had the two priests standing beside Father Johnson shivering out of control. Agent McKoy tapped Jack on the shoulder; her gentle touch seemed to calm his nerves.

"Father Andrew mentioned something about this transcendental stuff," Mullson highlighted Father Johnson.

"What transit stuff?" said Agent Hill, after noticing the two priests beside Father Johnson succumbed by fear.

Father Johnson sighed. "Transcendentalism," he said.

"Do you believe in transcendentalism?" Detective Mullson asked Father Johnson.

"Well," said Father Johnson. "It's a philosophy holding that ultimate reality is unknowable. One should assert the primacy of the spirit over the body."

"Can the spirit really dominate the body?" said Mullson, to Father Johnson. This had been bugging his mind ever since he ran into Engulf, without knowing it.

Agent Hill's face became reddened with frustration, his crooked brows frowned, and his eyes squinted almost out of control. "I refuse to listen to this nonsense!" he said.

"Anyone who speaks a word against the son of man, it will be forgiven, but to him who blasphemes against the Holy Spirit, it will not be forgiven!" Father Johnson cited from the bible, to Agent Hill. Father Johnson retrieved the lantern, shoved the door opened, and headed back in the direction they came. They all followed.

"Perhaps we're all a little frustrated," said Detective Mullson, to Father Johnson. "All day we had been searching for-"

"Ghost," Jack interrupted.

"A lot of questions and no answers," Agent McKoy pointed out to Father Johnson.

"You're not searching hard enough," Father Johnson told her. "Let's all forget about the physical objects."

"That will only complicate matters," Detective Mullson challenged Father Johnson.

"When you figure out the inner-man," whispered Father Johnson, "Then perhaps you might find the answer."

The helicopter had returned, Detective Mullson, Jack, Agent Hill, and McKoy tucked their heads into their chests and sprinted towards the chopper; they hurried inside, strapped themselves to their seats. Father Johnson and his two comrades stood by the church entrance waving goodbye as the helicopter rose and drifted away, until it disappeared.

CHAPTER 11

The moon shimmered red over house number nine hundred and ninety-nine, where inside the Mullson's living room the television volume drowned the sounds of a van, visible from the front windows, that had come and parked next to the mailbox. Johnny P, Murf, and Pain Killer were stretched out on the sofa focusing on the dazzling image of girls shaking their tail-feathers in one of the latest hip-hop videos making a buzz. They got so caught up they never noticed the assassin brothers who'd crept up to the front yard and scurried to the side of the house.

From next door Mrs. Newton continued to spy from her side window hoping the police would get to the Mullson's house in time to apprehend those burglars. Her dwindling mind had recalled seeing the tall black fellow coming to visit Anna on many occasions, but who cares. What worried her is the police hadn't shown up, after she'd called them so many times. This time she suspected something was terribly wrong, but because she'd abused her 911 privileges in the past...

She went and dialed the police for the tenth time, only now she planned to be more specific.

"Black kids are in the house!" she yelled over the phone then slammed it to the base.

Wait a minute, Mrs. Newton stretched her already long neck to get a good glimpse of the two fellows wearing black trench coats standing at the side of the Mullson's house, excitement rushed through her body, her first thought — police officers. Without warning her legs caved in and her lifeless body tumbled to the floor, after she spotted the two men gliding more than ten feet above the ground toward Anna's window.

Inside Anna's room the two Assassins searched every drawer and closet, under the bed, in the bathroom, behind the doors — whatever they sought they needed badly, for they kept clinching their fists and grinding their teeth. In the backdrop, the volume of the television lowered. Inside the living room Johnny P tossed the television remote aside, and could have sworn something ruffled within the house. "What's that?" he said, pulling out a .45 tucked away in his waist. He headed toward the dining room, slowly.

"What's what?" Murf asked.

"Told you to get real mother sucking gun padre," Pain Killer teased Johnny P.

"That's a real gun… Isn't it?" Murf questioned himself.

Pain Killer pulled out two M10s from under the sofa cushion where he sat and came swiftly toward the dining room. Johnny P accidentally brushed against Satan's knife sitting at the edge of the dining table. Pain Killer's finger twitched at the trigger, almost squeezing as he glimpsed the knife bounce against the floor.

Murf stood staring toward the dining room; behind him the two Assassins sneaked down the stairs and entered the living room. "Anything living kills it," said Pain Killer, staring at the strange knife. "If it's already dead, just kill it dead!"

"That's what am talking about my-" said Murf, his conversation ended when Assassin #1 threw a knife into the back of Murf's head, with the blade exiting the forehead, followed by a stream of blood spattering all over. Pain Killer glanced in the opposite direction and spotted Murf's body crashing against the floor.

The two assassins found themselves staring down the nozzle of the two submachine guns Pain Killer wheeled towards them; he pressed against the triggers —

In midair the two assassins rotated, jumped, dodged, tumbled — all at superhuman speed and outwitted every bullet inching away at them.

Johnny P swung around when he heard the thunderous booms and froze in his tracks at the sight of Murf lying in a pool of blood and the stunts the assassins were pulling off.

CLICK- CLICK-CLICK — Pain Killer continued to press the trigger, within seconds he'd emptied both clips. He tossed the M10s aside and pointed Johnny P to escape through the back door. "It not about BLACK, WHITE, HISPANIC…" he said, while blocking the entrance to the dining room.

"You're ma boy," Johnny P pleaded, "I'm not leaving you… yow, Pain Killer… let's go!" A strange look on Pain Killer's face had Johnny P wondering what Pain Killer was up to.

"Love you dog," Pain Killer told Johnny P, as if saying goodbye for the last time. "I'm doing this for Murf." He recalled forcing Murf to take the long ride from Brooklyn to Long Island; they'd come to retrieve one of Murf's recent creations which Johnny P accidentally gave to Anna. The plan was for them to open her window, pickup the sunglasses off a nightstand, and go. Now he regretted forcing them to stay for awhile.

Johnny P dived outside when Pain Killer flicked the pins from two grenades he took from under his clothing, just as the assassins were about to get a hold of him.

The whole neighborhood literally shook as two explosions rocked the dining room.

Pain Killer and Assassin #2 body parts scattered.

Assassin #1 used all his remaining strength and shoved away debris from his battered body; he dragged his carcass through the flaming house, all the way to the second floor where he glided from Anna's room window and landed next-door.

Officer Smith and Officer Brady from the Nassau PD were the only two who spotted the raggedy man gliding through the air, but they didn't alert their comrades, instead they turned away their heads and went to the back of the house. Outside the Mullson's house, Johnny P who'd come tumbling from inside tossed his gun aside as soon as he spotted police officers pointing their guns at him. Johnny P never did like the police much, but boy he was glad to see them. With a big grinned he dove to the ground, on his belly he laid with his hands extended outward. Officer Smith and Officer Brady jumped and braced against Johnny P's back as they slapped on the cuffs. Johnny P knew he was lucky to be alive; more than likely the police initially thought he was Detective Mullson who they had been warned to avoid.

"You got the wrong guy!" Johnny P kept yelling.

Officer Smith and Brady didn't like a bone in Johnny P black ass, only if they could pump a few rounds in him, they would be more than happy to send his miserable soul to the other side.

It had been thirty minutes since the fire department, located ten minutes away, was called, yet no sounds of their sirens wailed. The fire that had started in the dining room now spread throughout the house, finally reducing the place to rubbles and ashes.

Later that night a helicopter circling above remnants of the Mullson's residence began to dip lower and lower. Inside the helicopter, Detective Mullson, Jack, Agent Hill, and McKoy's faces appeared tense, their eyes weary, especially Mullson who was extremely worried about his wife and daughter in Jamaica. He'd no idea they were on the beach having a jolly time as the party cranked to the next level with line dances Anna and Mrs. Mullson had joined. A few planned visits had turned out to be a long day and now night of chases that led to nowhere.

Agent McKoy tapped Jack on the head.

"Is that your house, Jack?" she teased, jokingly, and had no clue whose house it was.

The Helicopter finally touched down in Mullson's neighborhood, but Mullson was not pleased to be home, his eyes widened and his strong square jaw dropped, as he stood before what was once his beautiful home.

"Where is my house?" he bellowed as he stumbled to his knees.

"We did absolutely everything in our power to save your house," said a chief from the fire department.

"I don't believe a word coming from their mouths," Agent McKoy whispered to Agent Hill, referring to the

people in charge of the investigation. Agent Hill acti-
vated the recording device on what appeared to be a
normal pen he placed in his shirt pocket, rolled up his
sleeves, then went and stood next to the officer in charge.
His intention was to gather all the information as to what
happened inside Mullson's home, the 911 call from the
late Mrs. Newton, the three introducers — yet nobody
mentioned anything about the fourth body they found
inside his home, the knife jammed through Murf's skull,
and a strange knife Officer Smith and Brady confiscated,
not listed as part of the evidence.

The whole thing reeked of lies, nothing seemed to add
up. Jack knew the truth after reading a few minds, for in
his head he heard voices — both alive and dead begging
for his mercy, but he must not risk revealing his true
identity — so he played on as a clueless human. The war
between heaven and earth had reached new heights, and
who's to become the don of hell had begun to take a toll
on the dark side, and that must get sorted out between
Satan and his son Engulf.

The Nassau County jail hadn't seen this much action
in one night, not as far as Sheriff Little-John could
remember, for he'd served two scores as of today. Within
the hour he expected to get a visit from an old pal he'd
work in the past with. He swung the back door open and
entered the staff parking lot. At an area shoved against the

wall, rested a few barbecues for the guards, below a sign bolted to the wall that read: Cafe Carucci.

From out of his pocket Sheriff Little-John ripped out a piece his father gave to him for his eighteenth birthday, a very special treasure the family had being handing down for generations, now the time had come for him to hand it to the next generation. The thought of his grandson flooded his mind.

"Perfect," he said with a husky voice, yanking his mustache. The Sheriff flipped the golden timepiece open and took a final glance as time ticked away; he snapped it shut before tossing the antique back into his pocket. In his mouth he stuck just the right amount of tobacco between his bottom lips and stained teeth. "I'll be damn."

Gaping into the night he girt the buckle of his belt, tucked in his belly, then released simultaneously as a big gulp of saliva glided across the parking lot. Sheriff Little-John drifted back to the door and disappeared into the building.

A few minutes later Mullson, Jack, Agent Hill, and Agent McKoy hurried across the parking lot towards the staff entrance of the Nassau County Jail. After getting off an elevator in a hallway lined with pastel green doors with black trim, they spotted Sheriff Little-John as he stood waiting for them.

"Welcome gentlemen," his hoarse voice echoed. "And madam. This is my home here at Nassau County... we have a closed door policy, if you get my drift." He pulled on his mustache and gave off a chuckle.

Agent Hill shook his pal's hand, been awhile since they'd last met.

"This is my partner Agent McKoy," Agent Hill pointed out to Sheriff Little-John. "Detective Mullson and Detective Jack from NYPD."

"Detective Mullson, and Detective Jack," said Sheriff Little-John, the smirk across his faced wiped away as he glanced at the two from the corner of his eyes. "We don't want any trouble here." He led them down the hall to the main cell block, consisting of four rows of grayish-white cells that seemed to go on forever. A second wall of bars separating the guard hallway from cells was barely big enough for one: each with its own toilet and sink, and a bunk bed against the wall opposite the sliding door.

At a door adjacent to the hallway Sheriff Little-John brought his guests to a standstill; he shoved a key in the hole and turned it clockwise. Detective Mullson and Agent McKoy entered a small room where a stench of musk hit their noses, at the center a table and three chairs stood in their perspective places, water condensed against the wall trickled to the concrete floor and settled at a spot where mold and mildew gathered.

At the table Johnny P sat with his head braced against his palms and hadn't said a word yet, sweat dribbled from his forehead, he drummed his knuckles on the table. He never cared much for Detective Mullson and Agent McKoy who stood in the room across from him and kept pressing him for stuff he'd nothing to do with.

Detective Mullson rushed over and clasped his hand around Johnny P's neck.

"Why… why?" he screamed at Johnny P.

Johnny P kicked and punched, but his eyes had begun to roll to the back of his head as he was succumb by Mullson's tightening grip.

Agent McKoy hurried over and forced Mullson to release the choke hold.

Johnny took a deep breath.

Mullson used his fist and delivered a crushing blow against the top of the table. "Why?" he said.

"I think we need to get Jack," Agent McKoy encouraged Mullson.

"I will take care of this myself," said Detective Mullson, to McKoy.

Johnny P was not down with all this poo poo nonsense, but what choice did he have getting blamed for a possible double homicide for his homies he loved dearly, arson, and burglary. With no alibi or evidence to clear his name he thought fast.

"Why don't you ask those cops about the others?" he finally blurted.

"Others?" said McKoy, confusion beaming across her face.

Through a glass partition, Detective Jack and Agent Hill stood staring into the interrogation room. The recording device was rolling.

"I don't know if I can trust him," Mullson told McKoy.

"What if he's telling the truth?" she whispered to Mullson, after pulling him aside to one corner of the room.

"I'm not lying man," Johnny P pleaded, "You can ask Anna. I gave her K Murder's sunglasses by accident. What about my boys. I lost everything…" All this he said quickly then banged his head against the table. "Everything!"

Mullson's interest peaked, it cannot be, how this scum bag knew his daughter. Did he go into her room and violate her belongings, read her mail, play the answering machine, all these thoughts raced through his mind.

"Murf — K Murder," he said.

"I took them from K Murder," said Johnny P, "But it belongs to Murf."

Jack and Agent Hill entered the interrogation room.

"Where is the knife?" Jack asked Johnny P.

After revelations as to what had happened at the Mullson's residence, and with possible leads regarding the mysterious knife found in Anna's room, and a description of the two men who killed Murf and K Murder, Mullson and his team finally got something to work with. They rushed along the hallway, until they reached the exit to the staff parking lot.

Mullson hopped into the driver's side of the Expedition while Jack secured the front passenger seat. Agent McKoy, driving the FBI sedan, tailed Mullson who'd sped away. This time the team hoped for a break, but all depends on the whereabouts of Officers Smith and Brady who they needed to answer some critical questions. Sheriff Little-John had no problem telling Agent Hill the duo's usual getaway — a small bar located a few miles west.

CHAPTER 12

A storm threatened over East Meadow Avenue — a small Long Island neighborhood attracted quite a few strangers for the past several hours, especially at the corner lot by the mortuary where Assassin #1 stood next to a USPS drop box, wearing a trench coat with burnt holes all over. He finally limped away and disappeared into the darkness. Usually all the buildings would have their lights turned off by eight o' clock, now it was well into the night, and from within the mortuary light was radiating from beyond the closed blinds.

Inside, a body bag was resting on a small table shoved against the wall adjacent to the front door, next to where Officer Smith and Brady stood waiting. At random both men walked back and forth and checked their timepieces for what must have been the millionth time.

The undertaker entered the lobby from a side door and came swiftly towards the two officers; his hands twittered out of control as he scanned the room, afterward, checked to make sure the door was locked.

"I will do the cremation as requested," he announced, ripping the bag open to look at the remains of Assassin #2.

Officer Smith shot him a wicked grin. "Good," he warned the undertaker. "Make sure you leave no clues."

The undertaker jammed a pen on a notepads. "Name and date of birth?" he said.

Officer Brady made a fist and smacked it against the palm of his other hand. "As my partner said," he reminded the undertaker. "No clues."

No sooner than the two men exited the building the undertaker slammed the door and turned the knob.

The rain was now drizzling as the two officers hurried towards a red pickup truck parked along the sidewalk, further down. The truck rumbled to life, the engine revved, tires squeaked against pavement as it raced down the street.

Officer Smith swung sharp on a side street and headed west; he speed up the wipers and stared through the windshield as the water slapped from the glass. He turned the radio to a channel playing heavy metal, and lowered the volume.

Brady had cracked the window to smoke a cigar, as he puffed he listened to the water hissing beneath the tires. He smiled as he picked up the knife they'd confiscated from the Mullson's home. What a beautiful piece, he thought. The craftsmanship beyond anything he'd ever seen, surviving both oxidization and abrasion from the fire.

Mullson and his team almost came to a crawl as they approached a saloon; observing the surroundings they spotted mostly bikes and oversized pickups scattered in the parking lot. At the door a giant of a fellow wearing a leather suit, stood with his arms folded and his fists clenched; he unfolded his arms to remove a cigar sticking from his mouth.

"We are here to see Officer Smith and Officer Brady," said Agent Hill to the man who blew smoke in their faces.

"Strangers are not welcome!" the big fellow bellowed, with a powerful bass.

"The pleasure is yours," said Agent Hill, stepping aside to let Jack handle the situation.

Jack grabbed the man by the balls and giggled; the fellow screamed in a high pitch voice and pointed towards the door for them to enter. After his colleagues all entered Jack remained outside, he had one more trick up his sleeve — he used one hand and hoisted the big fellow above the ground.

Inside, the scent of tobacco and whiskey tainted the air, but beneath lingered grunge and sweat. Some of the men hadn't seen water for days, judging by their filthy clothing. But that didn't prevent them from having a good time with plenty of sexy blondes to go around. Officer

Smith and Brady already got word of unwanted guests nosing about; they fled through an exit door leading to a parking lot further away at the side of the building.

Mullson got there in time and spotted the side door closing as if somebody just exited. They dashed towards the suspicious door.

Officer Smith's and Officer Brady's hearts raced as they pumped their arms and stretched their legs as fast as they could, and they were pretty fast, for in no time they reached a red pickup. Jack spotted the two officers and had begun to advance towards them when Mullson, Agent Hill, and Agent McKoy comes tumbling out of the bar.

Smith and Brady pulled their guns and fired, shattering windshields and setting off car alarms.

The few bystanders who thought the two police officers were being attacked got even more confused as Agent Hill and McKoy screamed, "FBI, get down!"

Mullson, Jack, Agent Hill and McKoy dodged behind parked vehicles.

More shots rang out; Mullson heard the whine of a bullet as it passed near his head.

"Hold your fire!"

The two continued to blast away before jumping into the pickup and sped away.

Mullson and his team scampered towards their vehicles, hurried in, and followed. Heading east at a section along Hempstead Turnpike, Mullson's Expedition and the

FBI Sedan with flashing lights trailed the red Pickup. Mullson gripped the steering wheel of the Expedition a little firmer as he glanced at the odometer creeping towards 110MPH, with Jack seated in the passenger seat staring at the pickup zigzagging ahead.

Inside the car, McKoy slammed her foot against the pedal. As she was about to pass the Expedition her attention was now focused on a Grumman Step Van heading in the opposite direction. Along the length of the van, as it darted by, she glimpsed flashes of the words 'I SCREAM.' Without warning she swung the car across the yellow line, cutting off oncoming traffic; the FBI sedan accelerated towards the 'I SCREAM' van.

Agent Hill clenched to his seat. "Wrong way!" he said.

"That's the truck," she tried to convince him.

"What truck?"

Agent McKoy pointed at the Grumman Step Van ahead whose driver refused to stop for the flashing lights.

Meanwhile, still heading east, Mullson's Expedition edged away at the red truck.

"Boring," Jack teased.

"Can you do better?" said Mullson.

Jack stuck his gun through the window, aimed at the back tires of the pickup, and fired two rounds that shattered the intended targets. With the two tires blown out, the truck hit an oncoming car, flipped several times before coming to a standstill on three wheels — the other wheel rolled down the street and crashed against a building. After radioing in an emergency Jack and Mullson came towards the pickup; inside they found the two officers' lifeless bodies.

On the seat of the truck Mullson spotted what appeared to be the knife his daughter had shown him earlier, he could have sworn, but he didn't want to get carried away. What if there were replicas floating around, or maybe the officers just didn't book all the evidence, what if they were covering up something. All these thoughts raced through his head, yet he didn't want to admit Johnny P might be telling the truth.

He lowered his hand to retrieve the knife, as he was about to get a grip of the handle, a dismantled hand lying on the floor suddenly came to life and grabbed a hold of his wrist. Mullson's heart raced, his mouth dropped, and the hair at the back of his neck rose. He tried to move, but his body didn't allow him to.

Jack had seen creepier stuff and didn't have a bone of scariness in him, all this excitement had his adrenaline double pacing; before Mullson had a chance to react Jack used his Glock and slammed a bullet into the revivified hand.

"Give me the knife," he said to Mullson. "At least it will be in the right hands."

Mullson swallowed. "Don't even say a word about this," he warned Jack, the whole thing gave him the creeps.

Along Hempstead Turnpike, the 'I SCREAM' truck sped toward Hicksville Road, a busy intersection ahead, where the stoplights turned red. A gasoline truck driving along Hicksville Road approached Hempstead Turnpike, a few meters away. The driver pressed against the accelerator and began to wind the steering counter clockwise when he spotted the green lights.

"Dad," said a little girl sitting on the front passenger seat, "are we there yet?"

"We'll be there soon," said the man. "Go get you some rest."

"Okay dad," said the little girl, rushing to a bed at the back of the semi.

"That's my girl."

The 'I SCREAM' Truck sped even faster as it neared the intersection; the light had been red for the past few seconds.

"Where are you guys?" Detective Mullson voiced echoed from the radio inside the FBI sedan, as McKoy and Hill saw the 'I SCREAM' van heading for an unavoidable collision with the gasoline truck. The Grumman Step Van smashed through the front of the gasoline truck.

Upon impact the tanker flipped to one side. The 'I SCREAM' van continued ahead in its original course.

Agent McKoy, seeing the accident, jammed on the brakes; the reaction sent the FBI Sedan plunging into the back of a garbage truck. It didn't take long for the hazmat team to arrive on the scene and had been slaving to contain the oil spill, after people were already forced to evacuate for miles. Detective Mullson, with blood all over his clothing, accompanied Agent Hill and the driver of the tanker into a hospital located on the outskirts of Hempstead; both men were in critical condition.

"Charl... Charlene," said the truck driver, gasping for air.

"Who is Charlene?" said a nurse. "Anyone know Charlene?"

"At the back, said the truck driver, his voice faded. "At the back of-" his heart monitor beeped as the line on the screen flattened.

"I think I know where to find her," Mullson whispered to himself, as he dashed toward the exit.

Detective Mullson raced to the intersection of Hicksville Road and Hempstead Turnpike and parked his Expedition a few blocks away. Toward the overturned truck he sprinted with all his might until he got to the scene where several firefighters apprehended him.

Foam covering vehicles and buildings was a temporary fix, most of the gasoline got vacuumed up by a tanker that had long gone. Wiring under the truck had begun to spark. "The truck goanna blow!" a firefighter yelled at the top of his lungs.

"A child is in that truck!" said Detective Mullson, struggling to set free.

"Impossible!" a second firefighter assured him.

"Give them the go ahead," the Captain told the first firefighter.

"Yes sir," he replied. Over his radio he shouted, "Evacuate the building!"

With the firefighter distracted Mullson set himself free; he scrambled on the truck, but there was no visible access to the cabin. He looked around and spotted a Firefighter Axe lying on the ground that he retrieved. The shirt Mullson ripped off from his body he used and wrapped around the head of the axe to cover up the metal area. He began to plow his way through the truck's roof, each hit had the potential for disaster, but a girl screaming from within the midst of the cabin encouraged him to work faster. The shirt fell off from the axe, but that didn't deter him. By the time Mullson got a grip of the little girl who'd being trapped inside a bed located at the back of the cabin, he was pretty much banged up. The place went up in flames. Explosions sent vehicles launching through the air. Firefighters retreated and shouted for Mullson to do the same, but it was too late as the flame engulfed him.

With almost nowhere to go he held on to Charlene and scanned the fire. Only if he'd listened to those firefighters who advised him not to endanger his life. Oh God he prayed, as tears of blood oozed down his cheeks, his final day had come. If he could only tell his wife and daughter how much he loves them, trying to save the girl was the right thing and not a thought of regret lurked in his mind.

A buzzing sound had him staring at the sky; a Rescue Helicopter hovered above the tanker, from the helicopter a rope came plummeting towards him.

"Hurry!" said Jack, from the back of the helicopter.

Mullson hugged the little girl tightly with one arm; he used the other hand and clinched the rope. The helicopter hauled them to safety, before the tanker shattered to pieces.

Outside Island hospital, a few miles away from the deadly accident scene, the National Guard had already begun to evacuate patients. A man in a wheelchair pedaled his way to a parking lot, the wheelchair got stuck in a pothole; the man made several attempts to free the wheels, but failed each time. He finally got up and sprinted away.

CHAPTER 13

The Big Apple had not seen this much action since 9/11, and nobody was more delighted than the news media who ran a story on every channel, analyzing and playing detective. The following morning when people woke it was only to learn of a serial killer on the loose and the massive explosion at the intersection of Hempstead Turnpike and Hicksville Road possibly linking to what had happened at the George Washington Bridge a few nights back. People were encouraged to walk in groups or if possible, not to go outside after dark. Regardless, New York City was open for business, only this time more police and undercover agents strolled the streets.

At a hospital, somewhere in Long Island, Agent Hill was still in a coma. A few of his colleagues who'd stop by the ICU headed out. At the outpatient area they entered a lobby where Agent McKoy sat in a wheelchair waiting. On her right hand she wore a cast; a nurse wheeled her towards the main lobby out front.

"I told you that van is responsible for all that mess," said Agent McKoy. All the other FBI members glanced at her; a cloud of doubt seemed to tamper their belief. "I'm sorry about Agent Hill," she continued. "It's my fault, but I'm not a liar." They entered the main lobby and exited.

At a Bronx Precinct, escorted by two officers, the deranged man was brought to the interrogation room and forced to sit at a table planted at the far corner. The two officers left when Mullson and Jack entered. The deranged man crumbled as he spotted the two.

Mullson had a rush of déjà vu and immediately sighed.

"Not again," he said, to the man whose identity was still unknown.

Jack held a picture of the prostitute before she got decapitated in Hunts Point.

"What a beauty," he said, slamming the picture against the table. "Did you love her?"

"I love you all," the mysterious man answered.

"Why did you kill her?" Jack accused.

"I could easily answer all your questions," the man bragged, "Even before asking, but life wouldn't be fun. Don't you agree Detective Jack?"

Mullson tossed a wallet before the man. The fellow scooped the wallet from the table. "It's about time you guys do your job," he said, as he got up to move toward the exit. Jack grabbed the man and flipped him high above the table and connected with a vicious blow to the man's chest. The man sprawled on top of the table. "Can I get up?" he mumbled.

"Go ahead," said Mullson.

The man jumped to his feet, stretched his arm towards Jack, and shuffled across the room. "Can I have a dance?" he asked Jack.

Jack glanced at him from head to toes. "Do you love your nuts?" he said.

"I'm longing to dance with the devil," the man teased Jack.

Mullson spotted Jack clenching his fist and rose above the head. "Jack!" he said, interrupting his motive. "Why are you here?" Mullson continued, to the man.

"Tricky question?" he turned and smiled at Mullson.

"Wrong answer," Jack threatened the fellow.

"I promise you this," said the man, to Mullson, trying to ignore Jack. "Whenever my mission is completed, if you wish, I'll be with you no more, but as for Jack, I'll be watching."

Mullson came and stood before the deranged man. "How do you explain the wallet?" he said to the fellow.

The man hesitated for a bit. "Since you insisted," he told Mullson. "I was robbed. I'm not the one you're looking for Detective Mullson."

"Get the Chief," said Mullson, to Jack.

Jack received and returned greetings as he strolled proudly along the first floor hallway. "A world without Jack is a dull world," he whispered to himself. "Don't you all agree?"

While Jack was scurrying along to the chief's office Mullson had something else in mind. First he wanted to know who he was up against, for the deranged man seemed to be hiding something or just playing dumb. From the interrogation room he stuck his head out and peeked into the hallway, both directions. As Mullson turned he found himself face-to-face with the deranged man.

"You and I have a score to settle," the man threatened.

Mullson used the index and thumb of his right hand and forced his wedding band further against his left-ring-finger. He slowly clinched both of his fists and punched several times toward the face of the deranged man who stood without even a blink. Mullson's hands were moving so fast they appeared blurry; a fist landed less than an inch away from the man's face.

"No name," said Detective Mullson, "no fingerprints, no family."

"You're all my family," the man bragged.

"Why are you always resisting?"

"You have to. If you don't you will ended up like the others."

"Is that a bad thing?"

"Depends on which side you're on."

"Let's go for a ride." Jack entered the room as Detective Mullson and the stranger were about to exit. "I will be back," said Mullson, to Jack.

"What should I tell the Chief?" said Jack, eyeing the deranged man.

"Anything," Mullson told him. "Just makes something up."

A well built woman, about mid-forties, entered. By the door she stood towering, her nametag read: JUSTICE. She scanned the room and spotted Jack bracing against the wall. "Detective Mullson!" she bellowed. She stared at Jack, "Where is that good for nothing bastard?" she continued, scurrying away when Jack's body expressions indicated he'd no clue about Mullson's whereabouts. "God, have mercy when I catch him."

Bums and drugs addicts roamed a side street where a black expedition sped along, slamming into potholes and running over garbage piled at random. From a distance a car trailed the expedition, inside the car Nina pressed the brake gently, coming to a standstill as she watched the SUV disappear out of sight.

Detective Mullson angled the Expedition to another street; through the rearview mirror he glanced at the deranged man who sat at the back.

"What if I am not on your side?" said Mullson.

"You're exactly what they're looking for," the man blurted. "The choice is yours."

"Should I believe all this nonsense?"

Mullson slammed on the brakes. He turned around, but the stranger had gone, almost as if vanished in thin air.

Detective Mullson searched inside the SUV, looked up and down the street, still no signs of the man. Using a hand he wiped away sweat gathering on his forehead, scanned his vehicle once more and discovered a ring on the backseat. He examined the ring, closely.

"You and I have a score to settle," the voice of the deranged man echoed in his head, as he recalled the incident in the interrogation room earlier. Mullson stared at his ring finger expecting to find his ring, but it was gone. He remembered threatening the man with his fast and furious fists, clenched fists, the thought of the man removing the ring from his clenched fist, disturbing.

"Oh my God," he whispered, as he slipped it on his ring finger.

At an abandoned warehouse at the edge of a small town parked several military looking vehicles. On the exterior of the building bricks were falling apart, the surroundings had shrubs popping up from cracks in the pavement, construction materials piled up in a far corner stood there for ages.

A hummer hurrying across an open lot came and parked at the front of the warehouse. Assassin #1 shoved the door open and leapt out of the driver's seat. He had on a black trench coat, this one free of burnt holes and rips. Engulf jumped out of the front passenger seat.

They headed towards a nearby door, and entered.

Inside the warehouse, a diverse group of men wearing black uniforms and well armed stood in a two-row formation, arms length away from each other. Engulf strolled back and forth inspecting his troops. "Failure is acceptable!" he said, with a wicked grin across his face.

"Never!" the troops said, proudly.

Ever since Mullson's house had been destroyed, Engulf found it difficult to keep an eye on the unpredictable bastard. In Jamaica his wife and daughter seemed safe, but not for long, Engulf thought. The grin disappeared from his face.

"We all deserve a vacation," he said. "I have the perfect place in mind."

"YES SIR… YES SIR!"

"Damn," Mullson muttered under his breath. A splitting headache hit him as he drove through an empty street after swinging to exit 7 off the Jersey Turnpike. He'd agreed to meet someone at Fort Dix about possible leads regarding the deadly assault on his former unit.

He pressed on the lever and stared as windshield washer fluid sprayed out and the wipers swished away the excess dirt. Well, he could only trust the person was not playing some sick prank. Mullson flipped on the radio and lowered the volume, his intent: the light music would smooth his headache. The thought of his family reminded him he needed to tell them about their house. He passed a cluster of plants at both sides of the road. Up ahead, closer to Route 537E, he planned to stop at Fowl Catcher Disco to get a drink.

As he drove along Route 537E his cellphone rang twice; he whisked it to his ear. "Where are you?" he said.

"Closer than you think," a male voice echoed from the other side. Several troopers' vehicles emerged from both sides of the cornfield. Mullson spotted them, and as they started to close in from all directions leaving him trapped, a sense of suspicion occupied his mind. He flashed his badge.

"NYPD!"

One of the troopers chuckled, Mullson recognized him from the crime scene at Liberty Street.

"You're out of your jurisdiction Detective Mullson," said Trooper Branson.

Mullson recalled hearing his voice before, wait a minute, the phone call. Oh no?

"You bastard!" he yelled, when he realized he was tricked. Mullson dived towards the front passenger door, busted it open then darted towards the cornfield.

A few troopers spotted their prey and gave chase.

With all his might Mullson trampled his way through the cornfield, not even the sharp edges of leaves slashing his arms slowed him.

In the backdrop an engine rumbled to life causing birds in nearby field to take to the sky.

Three troopers began to gain ground.

Mullson pushed harder and harder, until finally he outwitted his predators.

The earth trembled as a monster tractor came plowing through the cornfield — a Lexion 700 series pushing a twelve row maize harvester with the cutterbars blasting away at about 420rpm, cutting and threading everything in its path, more than thirty feet across.

Detective Mullson heard the thunderous roar that got louder and louder. Glancing over his shoulder he spotted a cloud of dust heading in his direction, quicker than his feet could carry him. His body continued to itch, sweat drenched his clothes, and the only things rushing through his head were the will to live and to see his family again.

With a sudden burst of energy Mullson thrust a little harder.

"No!" he bellowed, as his feet got stuck in what appeared to be quicksand. He stood still after discovering the chaotic movement only made him sink faster.

In the distance a person wearing a black ninja outfit stood tall, from beyond the mask both eyes fixed on Mullson, the handle of a sword jutted above the person's shoulder.

Mullson was now trapped between the ninja and the tractor that continued to advance from the opposite direction — he glanced at the harvester's blades and did not know what to do. The ninja, in midair, suddenly glided towards the tractor. The troopers, distracted by the ninja's action opened fire. The ninja tumbled—rotated—soared, and dodged every bullet headed in its direction, effortlessly.

Mullson finally dragged his carcass out of the puddle and found himself inches away from the blade of the harvester. With his eyes closed he curled up on the ground waiting to be devoured. The rumbling faded. Mullson got up to meet his maker, now afraid to open his eyes, and when he did he checked his body, all over.

"Am I dead?" he asked, patting himself again.

 Lucky for him the ninja had already slashed the driver in half with the deadly blade of a streaking sword, before turning off the monster. Everybody stared at the ninja who did a triple somersault from the tractor and landed below, on both feet. The ninja gripped a sphere, about half the size of a golf ball, and tossed it on the ground. A cloud of smoke erupted. The sounds of gunshot cuddled the air. When the smoke was cleared the person had long disappeared.

All the troopers who finally caught up realized this was no longer a joking matter. Now they were down one man, a good partner, they were surely going to miss him.

"Damn coward don't even have the guts to show his face!"

"He'll pay."

Six of them set out to track who was hiding behind the mask, gun in hands they were ready to tackle their mission. Kill, kill, and kill.

Four Troopers stayed behind to guard Detective Mullson: Trooper Branson held a shotgun in one hand, Trooper Keeley and Robeck dragged Mullson into the depth of the cornfield further away from the main road. Mullson struggled to set himself free but only received several kicks from Trooper Beasley. "Why can't you boys mind your own business?" said Beasley, teasing Mullson.

Meanwhile at another section of the cornfield the three troopers were still tracking the mysterious Ninja who emerged from underground, behind them. As the three men turned around to unload their weapons, the Ninja opened their stomachs with one blow as she pushed and pulled down on the blade. The troopers screamed as blood gushed from their guts.

Three other Troopers, who thought they were still on the trail of the Ninja, ran back toward the area where they heard their comrades wailing, but it was too late. They stood towering over their fallen comrades and had realized their secrets were no longer safe. A simple plan to get rid of Detective Mullson to protect the integrity of Joe and Benny had turnout to be a nightmare. They wondered who was the person wearing the ninja outfit. Professional killer? Jack? Got to be. Bastard. Wait a minute, he's not that short. Damn.

"There aint no way a sword should dee-flect all 'em bullets," one of the trooper blurted, sounding like a hillbilly. "Beyon' the laws of physics."

"What kind of sorcery is at work?"

"Well," a trooper who'd been silent finally spoke, "we all seen it." They knew what must be done. The hunt continued, this time a little more cautious, wheeling their weapons at every ruffle.

Mullson lied on his back in a puddle of blood. The four troopers, now wearing gas masks, stood over him. Two of the men began to rip off Mullson's clothing, everything, except for his underwear that he struggled to keep. All along Mullson had been squeezing his butt cheeks as he recalled watching his favorite movie — and he never did like the scene where a policeman kidnapped and raped a few fellows on their way through a small town — something fiction, but he'd no time to further contemplate.

Robeck pointed toward a hole in the ground, nearby. Piled inside were several corpses, including Mr. Rex's slightly decomposed body. "Get your clothes and don't come back around these parts, boy!" he said. Mullson peeped into the hole and spotted his pants and shirt; immediately he grabbed his nose and turned away as swarms of flies came pouring out.

Branson swung a leg and connected Mullson in the face.

From his eyes blood sprayed, and like a mighty titan Mullson's strength had returned. He tensed his body, waiting for the opportunity, as they let down their guard.

In a flash Mullson shattered Branson's leg, took away the shotgun then pumped bullets into the other three men. Their lifeless bodies hit the ground, for them the night had come quicker than they'd bargained — and their souls raced to join Joe and Benny — whether in heaven or hell, only God can tell.

Trooper Branson laid on the ground and screamed as the pain rattled his nerves.

"Please don't kill me," he pleaded to Mullson who stood over him pointing down the shotgun. "I don't want to die… I have a dog. "

Detective Mullson used his foot and shoved him in the hole.

The few cars and trucks traveling along a section of Route 537 halted as they spotted five state trooper vehicles surrounding a black SUV, blocking off the lanes in both direction. Ninja, sitting on Suzuki GSX 1300R Hayabusa, ripped off facial piece. The mysterious person was revealed to be Nina, the flight attendant Mullson had saved earlier.

She rode away into the evening, blasting along the desolated street, passing stretches of vegetation on both sides heading towards McGuire Air Force Base. She did her best to protect the man she'd falling in love with, the stranger who'd risked his life to save her. For that Nina was grateful. She somehow owed Mullson her life, but it's time for her to move on. She'd give him a fighting chance and hoped for him to survive his painful ordeal.

Nina shifted gears and almost maxed the Hayabusa that was traveling over two hundred miles per hour. A few minutes later she arrived at the Air Force base. After slipping into a change of clothing she hurried towards a military passenger plane and got on.

Mullson surveyed the cornfield and tried to map his way out. He had no idea his opponents were all dead, except Trooper Branson. Wearing only his underpants, and wheeling a shotgun he headed towards the center of the maize. Ahead, he spotted a car partially hidden, a black Benz with a license plate that read: MR REX. Mullson looked through the dark tinted window and jumped. At the back of the car a baby was strapped in her car seat; the skin had begun to melt from her body.

Mullson glanced at the sky as the sounds of a helicopter thundered. A FBI helicopter searched the cornfield below. Mullson was spotted and later escorted to safety, after Jack identified him as his partner.

Detective Mullson, wrapped in a blanket, stood by his SUV parked along Route 537.

Jack came and stood next to him.

"I'm sorry for not coming with-" he said, a rush of guilt dampened his face.

"It was my wish to go alone," Mullson interrupted.

Two FBI members followed Trooper Branson in the back of an ambulance before they whisked him off to the hospital.

The sun disappeared and night approached, the buzzing of insects filled the air.

Mullson was so grateful to be alive he'd forgotten he hadn't eaten all day. A text message alert made him jump, from under the blanket he brought a cellular phone he held in one hand before his face. The message came with the number 5555 attached. Mullson had no clue who sent him the text; over and over he read the words scrolling down the screen:

Congrats on your future endeavor…
hope happiness reigns between you and
your wife… you are a special man and
deserve every bit of it… God bless…
stay alive…

CHAPTER 14

A few days had passed, yet Mullson and his team got no closer to solving the mystery behind the senseless killing. With Agent Hill comatose and McKoy crippled by guilt, it was up to him and Jack to continue with the investigation.

In the Bronx at a park near Grace Avenue, Mullson sat on a bench staring at two teenage boys who stood opposite the park, on the right side of the road. Unusual warmth forced him to rip off his sweater and toss it on the bench.

"I stated clearly," Justice's voice echoed over the phone, "I'll address the issue as we speak— two of our finest officers are on their way. Mullson, Jack... we have a situation..."

The two had been assigned to stakeout the place for drug activities reported within the past few weeks — numerous complaints from concerned residents who threatened to relocate didn't sit well with the chief, not to mention the Mayor had a reelection to worry about.

"I understand you're in the middle of a crisis," said Justice. "I'm in the hot seat… scared away those thugs for a day… never came from me."

Justice had been covering up their destructive past for years, so it came as no surprise when Jack and Mullson agreed.

Inside the park Jack stood chitchatting with several females who were flattered by his handsome face and muscular physique. He sported a sleeveless shirt, a pair of shorts reaching his knees, the latest sneakers, and cool sunglasses hanging above his forehead. A Grumman step van approaching in the distance came and pulled up before the two boys.

Mullson's eyes flickered, like when his family is in danger or he was about to get bad news. He focused on 'I SCREAM' tattooed across the side of the van while digging deep to recall the name.

"Yes!" he said, jumping to his feet after remembering Agent McKoy's claim.

The two teenagers stood by a window watching.

"What can I get you fellows?" Wrath's voiced echoed from within the truck.

One of the boys threw up his two hands and began to exhibit some sort of gang signs.

"This truck is garbage," he blurted. "I don't see any ice cream. Where is the driver?"

"Fuck that nigga…" said the other boy. He hit the ground, as if something punched the light out of him.

The 'I SCREAM' van sped away.

At first Jack and Mullson sprinted towards the van, and as it began to slip away, they ran back towards their cars, and spotted the boy on the ground, unconscious. They tried to revitalize him. Mullson called in for backup when he realized the other boy had gone missing. By the time the investigation was over it was late into the evening. Jack and Mullson left the scene in separate cars; five minutes later they parked along a residential street and walked toward Mickle and Adee Avenue.

"That was the van," said Mullson.

"Maybe it's a replica." said Jack.

"Agent McKoy said she got evidence. We could give her a visit."

"We could, as in you and me?"

"What's wrong with that?"

"I need my privacy, you know the game."

"Which one?"

Jack twirled in the cool evening breeze. "How to be a player baby," he teased.

They giggled.

Mullson examined the corner he where thought he'd slammed his Porsche into a man; his attention was drawn to a feather twirling toward the ground, landing at his feet. He darted across the street and into the churchyard.

Jack, after staring at Mullson till he disappeared into the church, went and stood before a bar about two blocks away.

"Church is not my type of place," he whispered to himself.

Inside the church Father Andrew stood facing the pulpit. Detective Mullson walked toward him and halted a few feet away.

"I know you're probably busy," he said, followed by a long pause. "I need some information."

Father Andrew, still facing away, didn't say a word.

Detective Mullson had come to seek advice from the stubborn old priest who got him into the mess to begin with. Sure, he wanted was to shake the heck out of him and extract all the information he needed. Mullson sighed as he came towards the exit, uncertainty clouded his thoughts.

"Wait," said Father Andrew.

Mullson headed back towards Father Andrew.

"I need your help father," he said.

"Observe keenly," said Father Andrew, turning to face Mullson.

"I don't know what to believe anymore. I'm constantly bothered by nightmares."

Father Andrew went over to a window and peeped.

"Where's yer friend?" he said. Mullson seemed a little setback. "They're no difference from you and me," Father

Andrew continued. He walked back and forth almost to the same spot. "You failed to believe, even in the presence of God."

As night approached two priests who'd come out to close the church, decided to hold off, giving Mullson more time to redeem his soul.

Father Andrew drifted closer towards the two men who'd been ignoring him for almost two years. Ever since his encounter on a roof in New York during a particular stormy night things hadn't been the same. "I could have told you that you're not welcome in the house of God," he said to Mullson, "just as he is not welcome in yours. Never underestimate the little people Detective Mullson."

"What am I supposed to do?" said Mullson, looking uncertain.

"The answer lies within you," said Father Andrew.

Mullson's mind had begun to wander — he somehow cannot get these images out of his head: it all happened a few weeks ago, after he'd come back from Africa. Inside a hotel room candlelight flickered to give the room an orange glow; with a touch of sensuality the aroma of roses and amber filled the air. Two people covered from head to toe, and indulged in their sexual fantasy, moaned and groaned as they kissed each other. "It's not right," a male said, as he flung the cover aside exposing Nina and Mullson cuddled up in bed, fully dressed.

"I'm so sorry," said Nina, hopping off the bed. She flicked on the light and the room was brightened. "Hope you forgive me."

On one side of the bed Mullson sat facing away, "Please don't blame yourself," he pleaded. "Just some personal issue I need to straighten out, hope you'll understand."

"A dark cloud is hanging over my faith," Mullson admitted, to Father Andrew, thinking about what had happened, and the shame raging through his heart. He loves his wife dearly. How could he?

It was late into the evening when Father Andrew and Detective Mullson went and stood in the church parking lot, next to Mullson's parked Expedition.

"If one builds on their mistakes," said Father Andrew, off the top of his head "I can assume one is of good character."

Mullson scratched his chin and stood silent for awhile. "Remember the gentleman I confronted on the plane?" he said, finally getting it off his chest.

"The one you almost killed?" Father Andrew gave out.

"Who is he?"

"Whatever happens, be there for your son in law."

Mullson bit down hard on his lower lip and clenched his fist.

"He is not my son in law for heaven sake!"

"Anna made that choice Detective Mullson. Destiny is nothing but chance. Unity is the only medicine to defeat evil!"

"Who's he?"

"When the time is right he will appear like a thief in the night…"

They walked swiftly toward the exit.

Outside they got distracted by a limousine driving along Mickle Avenue, at the outer perimeter of the rear parking lot where they stood. The rear window of the limousine rolled down slowly and revealed a headless person. The upper body had on a sport jacket.

Mullson blinked twice then rubbed his eyes. Father Andrew gave him a light tap on the shoulder to assure him he wasn't going crazy. The headless man, whose head was now reformed in the image of what was seemingly Detective Mullson, stuck out his middle finger at the two.

Mullson dashed toward the limo as it raced toward the end of Mickle Avenue and angled a sharp right at Arnow Avenue; he stared at the limo till it was out of sight. He came back and stood near Father Andrew.

"What have I done to deserve this?" he said.

"That wasn't your fault Detective Mullson," said Father Andrew. "Crying will not bring your brother back." He shuffled his feet and whispered. "Can you tell the difference between the dead or the living?"

Father Andrew held his head and screamed as his eyes flipped and ballooned, almost about to explode, his world consumed by darkness followed by a sense of forward movement between time and space through what appeared to be a wormhole. At the end of the tunnel Father Andrew glimpsed a river — a girl was in danger; she resembled the person who'd come to the airport to pick up Detective Mullson. He'd no idea he witnessed the future — a split second — the war had been picking up pace. He tried to warn Mullson before going into a seizure.

Mullson checked Father Andrew's vital signs. At first he detected no pulse or heartbeat. One-two-three — he pumped against Father Andrews's chest and listened for the slightest flicker... One-two-three, he repeated two more times, till at last... He heaved a sigh of relief.

Mullson couldn't muster any help from the two priests who'd come outside and seemingly showed no interest in Father Andrew's well being. He hoisted Father Andrew over his shoulder and carried him all the way to the front, up a few steps, and into the church; he hadn't give much thought to how weightless Father Andrew's body felt, almost like a feather.

Inside he placed him on a blanket spread out on the ground. Later into the night Father Johnson and another priest arrived. Detective Mullson kneeled over Father

Andrew. The four priests including Father Johnson prayed.

Father Andrew sparkled back to life, after his soul exited the wormhole, yet nobody other than Detective Mullson showed interest.

"She is in great danger," his faint voice warned Mullson.

"Father Andrew," an excited Mullson said, "you're alive." Three of the priests, excluding Father Johnson, glanced at Detective Mullson. Now they thought he needed some serious psychological attention.

"Great danger," he said to Mullson, his voice sluggish. "You must go now."

Nothing was unusual about the crowd merging towards the Sheraton Hotel, Seventh Avenue, New York, except for a few undercover agents from the FBI and the military blending in with civilians, all units with their own agendas, and independent of the others.

Agent McKoy was the only occupant in the room at number six hundred and sixty-seven, at least that's what she thought. She stared at her handbag resting on the bed with the contents spilling, next to a handgun. The sheets crumpled and tossed aside, the television on with the volume lowered to almost a whisper, a clock radio on a nightstand showed the digital time: 5:00.

She'd one hand in a cast below the elbow secured by a sling; the other hand she used to help slide her tight shorts over her naked thighs, down her two long and luscious legs. McKoy shuffled toward the bathroom, each step with excruciating pain, as she gripped a fist and bit down on her teeth. Before entering the bathroom she glanced over her shoulders and could have sworn someone had being stalking her. Well, she thought her imagination — a little uncanny, blaming it on the lack of sleep ever since the accident.

Agent Hill had being creeping between life and death, literally. While his body laid in the coma his spirit was elsewhere. Two nurses who'd been observing him seemed confused as the heartbeat monitor became strangely unstable. "Get the doctor," one of the women said, banging against the monitor. The other nurse rushed out of the room —

Agent McKoy was surprised at how jumpy she was when she thought she'd seen Agent Hill lingering around the room when she dreamed, during her private moments after exiting the shower. She wiped away most of the water running down her curvy figure, except for her back which was painful to reach. Over her body she sprayed her favorite perfume smelling the sweet and sexy scent — a little overwhelming in the humid air. McKoy gazed back at her reflection in the mirror, using the fingers of her freed hand she poked around the bags drooping below her eyes.

By the toilet she stooped and retrieved a small diskette she'd earlier hidden behind the tank. From a small bottle she poured out a liquid substance that fizzed when it touched her cast; Agent McKoy carved her way into the eaten away section of her cast and secured the diskette inside. Afterwards, she smoothed and blended the surface.

Meanwhile in room six hundred and sixty-eight, a black fellow lowered his shoulder to fit his tall frame in the bathroom mirror. He had on a black tuxedo along with a pair of white gloves. The man kept nodding his head in disapproval as he observed his face, keenly. He began to scratch his face, faster and faster, but the itchy sensation wouldn't go away. The man slapped both sides of his jaw, extremely hard. He peeled away a layer of skin; rotten flesh filled with pus seeped down his charred face exposing his true identity. From a bottle containing rubbing alcohol he poured a handful and daubed his face till the worms itching away under his skin slithered to the surface, curled up and fell into the sink.

Wrath advanced towards the bedroom and began to search through a variety of facial masks stuffed in a suitcase lying on top of the bed. A clock radio resting on top of a nightstand showed the time: 5:01. He picked up a mask and hurried back to the bathroom, in the meantime slipping the mask over his face; his hairpiece shifted to one side of his head during the process. He stared in the mirror for quite awhile, secured his wig, knotted his tie. His eyes widened with satisfaction as he curled his toes in his spit-polished alligator boots. A slow smile spread across his face.

"What a handsome man," he squeaked.

He had a close resemblance of Detective Mullson — his old self indeed, but he was not the same person. His blood pressure spiked. Daniel was dead and he knew it. His thirst went unquenched in his quest to redeem his mortal spirit; a man of adventurous intent had been succumbed by exhaustion from battling his demons, now beyond his control.

CHAPTER 15

In Montego Bay, Jamaica a cool breeze rushed across the land ruffling tree branches and had the grass swaying to and fro, carrying the odor of ripe mangoes along. The sun that had been dipping beyond the horizon painted the clouds orange, red, blue and white, like a splash tie dye.

Anna, wearing sweatpants and a T-shirt, wandered across the luscious countryside and spotted a small river ahead. Her imagination was enthralled as she trailed the waterway, looking at exotic birds, animals and vegetation, all arrayed by nature for her viewing pleasure. As she approached a section of the river three boys spotted her and dodged behind a patch of bushes, peeping at her.

At the riverbank Anna stooped and began to swoosh her fingers through the crystal clear water. She recalled her mother warning, "Don't go venturing off alone," but how can a person resist such allure. After all, in Long Island she'd none of these things to cherish. Reflecting on the book 'Barefoot, Prickles, and Thorns' gave her goosebumps, the vivid scenery as she'd pictured Jamaica — in no way shy of the beautiful paradise the book described.

Anna lost her balance and as she was about to fall into the water, she used the strength from one hand and swung her body, landing on her butt instead of her face. The boys giggled aloud when they spotted her. Anna immediately scanned the area she thought she heard laughers erupting, but the reverberation in the backdrop had her tricked. In the shallow she sat laughing as she finally glimpsed three little heads peeping at her from behind some shrubs.

The boys, about six years old at most, came out into the open. With their hands covering their private parts the naked three ran and tumbled in the river, splashing water all over Anna, messing up her recent hair do, but that didn't dampen her spirit as she enjoyed the playful moment. It was kind of weird for her as she experienced children hanging out at a river without adult supervision and no swim trunks. This is what you call a free country, amazing.

The day had been drifting and Anna barely noticed darkness descending, or how worried her mother must have being. The boys were no longer in any mood to play. They seemed hollowed, as if she was looking through glass.

"You must go now," the first boy warned Anna.

"What's wrong?" said Anna.

"You're in danger," said the second boy in a faint voice.

"Go now," the third boy bellowed, "now!" his voice sounded more croaky than that of a grown man.

A terrified Anna jumped to her feet and stared at the three boys who'd begun to vanish. Realizing the boys were ghosts she hustled towards the center of the river. Thunder rumbled, louder this time. The rain had started, soft at first. She felt the cool breeze picking up speed.

An old lady with a rod appeared on the bank of the river — the side Anna needed to get to on her way home. The woman was covered from head to toes in a black raggedy gown; her eyes glowed in the unusual darkness. The wind gusts were strong now, and the bushes swayed back and forth, dancing strangely in the moonlight. She stared at Anna.

Anna stared back. Her skin cold, prickly goose bumps raced up her arms, splashing across her neck. As the moon exited a dark cloud, its light gleamed across the woman's face. She looked familiar, Anna remembered quite well. The old lady was a spitting resemblance of the transformed image of Annie Palmer, the one she spotted on the picture during her brief encounter at Rose Hall.

Anna twisted and turned, over and over, but she could not move her legs. The only thing that came to her naturally was to scream at the top of her lungs. She did, but nobody came to help. She looked down at the water as it changed to blood red. Grabbing her throat she gasped for air, a bitter taste filled her mouth and she began to spit froth. Again she tried to scream, but managed only a few crackles. She twisted and turned, still she could not move.

A tunnel formed in the clouds looming above.

Anna spotted it. The old lady dipped her rod into the river and shook out of control as if being electrocuted. The water changed back from red to neutral, the sky brightened to reveal sundown, and the wind became calm.

"Get out of the water," her squeaky voice echoed. "Run for your life!"

Anna tugged her legs once more and moved hurriedly towards the bank. The old lady's eyeballs suddenly popped out off her head; with all of her energy used up she hit the ground with a thud. Anna got even more scared, but didn't want to leave the poor lady by herself. She went and stooped over her, but ran away screaming as she spotted the mummified remains of the old lady that had two giant centipedes crawling out of the eye sockets.

On top of a hill a small house stood alone. Nearby, an outline of trees and shrubs danced in the evening wind. At the backyard, two mongrels chased some chickens that had missed landing on their roosts on a nearby cotton tree. The chickens finally got to their destination. The mongrels scampered to the front of the yard and stood howling at Mrs. Mullson.

On a chair against the wall she sat on the porch staring into the distance, watching the birds hovering above, and colorful streaks painted the sky as the sun had begun to dip beyond the horizon. A sudden rush of wind caught her off guard, but the gust deadened upon arrival.

"Mother!" she said.

"What you want Mrs. Mullson?" asked a lady with a heavy Jamaican accent, from inside of the house. She came and stood on the porch next to Mrs. Mullson; she was early sixties with grayish-black hair drooping to her shoulder.

"Where is my baby?" Mrs. Mullson asked her mother, referring to Anna.

From the midst of the house the telephone rang twice. Magarette rushed inside and whisked the phone to her ears. "Hello," she said, before bursting into tears. "I don't know where she is."

"Get in contact with the police," said Trevor Mullson. "If I have to pay, just do it."

Magarette had a burning sensation piercing her stomach — maybe the jerked chicken, she thought, or those spicy patties she ate earlier, damn. "Hold up," she said-

"Grab everybody and go to the church… you will be safe there… tell Pastor James I sent you… don't move until I get there," Detective Mullson said all these in a hurry.

"Here we go again, telling me how to spend my vacation," said Magarette. "If it was not for your selfishness this wouldn't be happening in the first place."

Somewhere along Seventh Avenue Mullson stood by a pay phone conversing.

"Hold on, hold on…" he said. "Please don't hang…" He listened as the phone slammed from the other side and the dial tone echoed. In his quest to get to the other side of the street, he darted towards the yellow line, dodged and jumped to avoid oncoming traffic, till he reached his destination. He was hurrying to get to his partner Jack who'd being waiting in Central Park.

The guilt of putting his family in danger had begun to take a toll on him, what could have possibly went wrong for he hadn't seen it coming. He thought about all the names of dangerous people he stuck behind bars, but none rang a bell. Some psychopath was stalking him, and he wished he knew who. If he could put his hands around the sumbitch's neck, damn he wanted to squeezed the heck of him. Get a grip of yourself Mullson, come-on. He took a deep breath and exhaled.

At Central Park Jack sat on a bench skimming through a newspaper, every once in a while he stared into the night, but there was nothing much to see, other than joggers, snooty ladies walking their dogs, a few fellows that gave him the creeps, a blonde with long solid legs — finally. He tossed the paper aside, rubbing his palms together he watched as the lady glided in his direction, so perfect in her short pink dress and a pair of high heels.

As the lady, looking absolutely gorgeous in every manner, went by Jack waved.

"What's up babe?" he said, with a grin across his face. He undressed the lady with his eyes, observing her from head to toe. He reminded himself he is an officer and should live by a higher standard, thus allowing his stuff to shrivel back to the dormant position.

The blonde passed and glanced back to check out the cute fellow who'd just waved — the accent as he pronounced "babe" stirred up something under her dress. Her nipples hardened, she used a hand to grab the oversized clit poking through her favorite rainbow colored thong, as she pretended to be straightening the front of her dress. She'd been so excited, so thrilled; she couldn't resist the sexy Italian stud...

"Hello miss thing," she said, with a hoarse male voice.

Jack almost jumped out of his pants. "Holly shit!" he said to himself. "No more pretty girl for Jack."

Before the Sheraton Hotel a black Expedition came and stopped; Mullson and Father Johnson hopped out and scurried toward the entrance. The lobby was crammed with people entering and leaving, door men and greeters kept smiling, bellboys dragged luggage behind guests who accepted their help. At one corner Jack and Captain Austin sat waiting, when they spotted Mullson and Father Johnson rushing toward the front desk, they got up and joined them.

"Where can I find Miss McKoy?" Detective Mullson interrupted a clerk who cracked a smiled as he get ready to greet them.

"What is your name sir?" said the clerk, rushing over a guest list. Mullson flashed his badge; the clerk looked at him. "You already checked in earlier-" he said.

"Which room?" Mullson yelled.

"Six-six-seven," said the clerk, his hands trembling out of control.

On the sixth floor Mullson and Jack exited the elevator and entered the long stretch of hallway, hurrying along till they reached room 667 where they stopped and found the door ajar. Mullson tapped on the door. Inside the room the television was on with the volume set to low, the wall opposite the door was totally covered with mirrors. Mullson glanced into the mirrors and noticed the place had being torn apart, as if a storm had passed through. The mattress tossed to the floor, all drawers ripped from their units and their contents scattered.

They drew their weapons and entered, walking slowly as they scanned their surroundings. Jack spotted a gun partially hidden by the mattress.

"Agent McKoy!" he said, as he used a finger to knock the mattress aside like a toothpick, not remembering his partner was present. "Agent McKoy!"

Mullson could have sworn the mattress sailed across the room; he rubbed his eyes. "I'm losing it," he whispered to himself, after staring at the mattress now back in its original spot, within a blink.

A clock radio resting on top of the nightstand indicated the time was now 8:00.

Jack picked up the gun and observed it. "Nice cologne," he said, after sniffing the air.

"Deep secrets," said Mullson.

Both men rushed toward the bathroom and shoved the half open door; they crept into the bathroom where they found Agent McKoy sprawled out on the floor with her throat busted open, inside painted red with blood.

Mullson dropped to his knees and began to check Agent McKoy's nose, neck, and wrists. He dialed his phone and yelled, "Hurry!"

Jack had never cried all his life and when tears trickled down his face the heaven smiled, as ruthless as he'd been there was hope. In the bedroom he came and crumpled in a corner. "I promise I will find the person who did this," he told himself.

On Agent McKoy's cast Detective Mullson spotted the initial 'AH' scribbled in blood. "A.H.," he said, picking his brain, "Air Hostess, Agent Hill- what am I thinking?"

He went and joined Jack; they exited into the hallway, further ahead made a sharp right. Before they reach the elevator Mullson spun around and ran back in the direction he came, toward room 667. Jack stared at Mullson and wondered what he was up to. Mullson dashed through the front door, and into the bathroom where he checked the cast on Agent McKoy's hand. He peeled away a portion of the cast next to the bloody initials and removed a small diskette, as if by instinct. On his way out he stopped short of the exit door that had now been closed; as he grasped the handle of the door to open it hundreds of tiny pins emerged from the mirrors and rocketed toward him. Like a well trained monk he dodged and glanced at the pins as they went by him and stuck in the back of the door.

A ninja in a suit made of mirrors emerged from the wall mirrors and attacked Detective Mullson who possesses some acrobatic skills. He fended off the ninja who refused to give up. Mullson, flying through the air, broke his falls on the mattress lying on the ground. The ninja used trickery to gain the final advantage by frequently disappearing back and forth in and out of the wall mirror. Mullson scanned the room; this time the ninja had disappeared longer than usual.

In the hallway Jack sniffed his way to room 667 and found the door closed, as he raised his hand to knock his sixth sense tickled. He worked his way to room 668 where he placed an ear against the door and listened to the ticking of a timepiece, and the flushing of a toilet in the backdrop.

Inside room 668, Wrath's suitcase stuffed with masks lay on the bed, a pocket watch and a wallet rested on a nightstand, next to a clock radio. The sounds of the toilet being flushed echoed. Wrath, in his new identity, exited the bathroom and came towards the room. He examined the place after smelling the present of someone. Not just anyone. The person or thing he sensed made him nervous; he figured it wasn't Engulf, nonetheless he felt just as scared.

Jack continued to press his ear against door and sensed the presence of something unusual, a person for sure, yet no heartbeat. This can't be real, he reminded himself. Whatever was lurking behind the door he needed to know. His anxious mind couldn't wait any longer; he lowered his hand and grabbed the handle, bracing his body against the door. But the door didn't budge. He raised a foot with the intent to kick the door off its hinges.

Wrath opened his mouth as wide as he could. "AAAAARRRRRRGH!" he thundered a high pitch scream that shattered windows, mirrors, and other glass objects, before Jack's foot came crashing through the door.

Jack's eyes scanned the room for the slightest of movement; a reek of cologne hit his nose, a brand he recognized, Detective Mullson's favorite. Other than a few unwanted items lingering around there was not much to see. The person who he thought was in the room had long gone. By the window he stood looking at the street below and got a glimpse of a man plummeting from next door — the man was wearing only a pair of underwear. He knew the man was not from this world, for he'd disappeared just before hitting the ground. Engulf had something to do with this, he reminded himself, as he dashed out of the room to go and check his partner next door.

Earlier in room 667: broken mirrors scattered on the floor, mostly by the wall where they'd been plastered over, the window frame stood without the two-inch thick glass that was originally there. Wearing only a pair of underwear, Assassin #1 stood defenseless by the window whose glass had crashed on the street below. The Assassin had being stunned for a moment; as soon as he got a grip of himself he dived through the window.

Mullson rushed over and peeped, expecting a pulp of a body lying in the street below. He'd seen many suicides where people jumped off buildings, bridges, blew out their brains, but none like this, where windows shattered on their own and a naked man jumped from a sixth floor room— but the stranger was not there. He stared at the street, more intensely than ever. What on God's earth is going on? A cloud of doubt flushed his mind, but how could he be seeing things, the window was broken, not your typical glass window, had to be bullet proof, a few inches thick.

On the first floor Captain Austin and Father Johnson stood waiting in the crowded lobby. They kept staring at the elevators whenever the doors opened and people got off.

"I'm going up," said Captain Austin, to Father Johnson, moving towards the elevator.

"Not yet my son," said Father Johnson.

On the sixth floor NYPD rushed out of the elevators; Captain Austin followed closely.

CHAPTER 16

I t was late into the night when a military plane jetted across the overcast sky, the pilot took extra care to evade the airspace closer to Cuba. Mullson, Jack, Johnny P, Father Johnson, and Captain Austin were aboard with parachute packs strapped to their backs. Captain Austin stuffed a German M-42 Machine Gun, a few high power riffles, M16s, and bow and arrows into a duffle bag. A smirk across his face was masked beneath his sturdy looks as he eyed two soldiers screaming at Johnny P.

"Extend your arms and try to keep calm."

"That will help with your balance."

"Use your flashlight to check to make sure your canopy is properly deployed. Remember the Dark Zone."

"What?"

"Above one hundred feet you will see the landing zone!"

"Once you get close to the ground, the ambient light source is lost, because of the low angle of reflection. Below one hundred feet it becomes very dark, and you hit the ground soon after."

"The ground rush is wicked!"

"Soldiers, you are trained. Your weapon is your buddy, never leave your buddy behind!"

All the tips didn't keep Johnny P from wanting to go on himself, his legs got so weak he barely could walk, he'd agreed to go along to help rescue Anna, but he never bargained to jump out of a moving plane — the last time he remembered he was afraid of flying. I'll do whatever it takes to save my girl, he repeated in his mind, over and over.

Detective Mullson went and stood next to Father Johnson. "How this madness got started?" he asked.

Father Johnson took a deep breath then exhaled. "Engulf made a deal with the Klan to preserved the soul of fallen Klan members," he said, followed by a long paused.

"How does that fit into the puzzle?" said Mullson.

"One night one of Engulf's best disciples was terminated somewhere in Africa," said a convincing sounding Father Johnson. "As a means of revenge, Engulf ordered the soul of fallen Klan members to devour the body of many black youths."

Johnny P had being worrying about the mission, his two pals Murf and Pain Killer who'd left him too soon, and now he hopes his girlfriend was safe. His attention got drifted abit when he overheard what Father Johnson told Detective Mullson. "That explains why niggers kill each other," he blurted. All eyes gazed at him. "What?"

Jack who'd been quiet all along and tucked away at the back finally got up; he went and joined the rest of his team closer to the center of the plane. "Children these days," he said to Father Johnson. "How sad."

Captain Austin had a light grin across his face, to be in control gave him the utmost pleasure, like telling people when to move, stand, sit, eat, speak, even convincing the pilot to let him off in the Caribbean. The marines had made a man out of him, but those good old days had being fading as the years withered. He'd recently discovered the enemies who were responsible for the death of his fellow marines had being lurking somewhere in Jamaica. How dare those bastards, his blood pressure peaked on the high side — after a deep breath it normalized. Whatever Captain Austin wants he gets, nothing would sooth him more than killing the vacation of those cowards he seeks. But how could they challenged my marines and live, a thought flashed in his head. Are they aliens from another planet, possible super human, nonsense. God help those bastards when I get my marine's hand around their throats and squeeze every breath out of their measly bodies.

"What exactly are we up against?" he said to Father Johnson whose mind had being busy asking God for help.

"Trust me," said Jack, to Captain Austin. "You don't want to know."

"We all have our purpose," said Father Johnson, to Captain Austin. "Don't be discouraged.

As the plane drew closer to the drop zone Mullson thought about some of the risk factors he'd encountered during those years he spent in the marines, like getting tangled in someone else's chute. With the plane running into some turbulence he figured it would be best for him to make the jump alone, he'd done this hundreds of time and knew what to do if he get caught in the downdrafts closer to the ground. Now that the wind had being calmed for the past few minutes Mullson had one less thing to worry about. "Hope everyone is ready for action," he said, as the plane flew over the island nation of Jamaica.

Johnny P had advanced further into the woods, other than been told he landed in Montego Bay he'd no idea where he stood. With one hand griping a German MG 42 machine gun close to his body, and a chain of bullets tossed over one shoulder for support, he used the light beaming from his flashlight to scan his surroundings, before moving in the opposite direction. "Remember to be vigilant," Mullson had warned him, "Your vacation starts after we find Anna. Stay close to the group."

Finally, the morning came alive with the buzzing of insects, the barking of dogs echoed nearby, the unsettling of fowl, crabs slithering over dried leaves to the nearest hole disappearing with a splash. The sun emerging from beyond the hill had begun to glitter through branches. Dew collected on leaves and spider's webs lied undisturbed.

With both hands gripping the machine gun Johnny P stopped and aimed when he heard ruffles ahead. Sweat condensing on his forehead trickled to his mouth; he licked his lips.

"Who goes there!" he said, and when he got no reply he pressed the trigger. His eyes widened with amazement as bullets riddled leaves and branches. The kick had a sensation he'd never experienced before, more delightful than a kid in a candy store, whatever he was going through felt great, almost as if he'd became invincible.

A faint scream had him convinced the intruder had fallen; Johnny P came and stumbled upon a body threaded apart by the 57mm JS cartridge of the MG 42.

The weary sound of a goat expired its last breathe.

"Damn," he said, using one hand and covered his mouth as the sight of the blood turned his stomach. He spun around and spotted a person dodging behind a patch of bushes. The fellow who sported a black trench coat resembled the man Pain Killer had blown to pieces.

"Juliet, over!" Mullson's voice echoed from a two way radio tucked away in one of Johnny's pocket.

After what seemed like a dead-end chase Detective Mullson finally took a breather, he focused on a patch of shrubs that had a cluster of ticks crawling about; he tucked his khaki pants into his boots and the khaki shirt into his pants. Across one shoulder he secured a M16-A2 rifle, picked up his bow and arrows that had being resting on the ground. Mullson placed a pair of sunglasses over his eyes that showed a computerized screen with what appears to be a map of the surrounding area.

"Location of closest human object," he demanded and stared at hundreds of words zooming across the screen followed by the plotting of several grid points. RESULTS: 0.5 miles radius, closest human object.

A slithering sound made him freeze where he stood pointing the rifle ahead.

A bush near a cleared section quivered... Jack came stalling into the open, and almost tripped over the remains of a rotten tree; he moved swiftly toward Mullson and just realized he was staring down the barrel of a gun.

"That's impossible," said Mullson, still pointing the gun at Jack.

"Not so fast mister," Jack warned him.

"Changed your mind?"

"I don't need a weapon to survive." Jack used his hands and ran over the formal attires he sported. "I am the man, you know me."

Detective Mullson finally pointed away the M16.

"You said so. I never managed to get a grid on you."

"Technology," said Jack, after stalling for awhile. "Never put your trust in them."

"Let's go."

Mullson headed in the direction of a point he randomly selected from the grid displaying before his eyes. Jack followed. They came toward a river; when they got to the bank they discovered the remains of a skeleton, Mullson observed keenly, but nothing was adding up, the body didn't resemble anything he'd previously tackled for forensic evidence.

Jack recognized the soul he'd encountered in the distant past, not your typical girl, yes indeed, Annie Palmer was one hot tempered brunet, in the bedroom skillful and accommodating. Jack reflected on good old days, to him a century seems like yesterday. How her body got here puzzled him a lot. What is going on, who's in charge? Jack thought to himself. He studied the area and spotted one foot of a flip-flop hidden among the grass, footprints pointing towards a wooded section, further along the trail was the matching flip-flop followed by two drag marks in the mud.

Mullson's heart raced after suspecting the slippers belonged to Anna.

"Oh my God please make her be okay," he said. "What if something happened to my baby?"

"She's still alive," Jack assured him.

All the thoughts rushing through Mullson's head seized for a brief moment. With the exception for tasteful women and religious creed Jack had always being right about most things; Mullson found comfort in his word and got a grip of himself.

Almost thirty minutes had passed and the track suddenly went cold, a rocky area ahead had left no clues, where Jack and Mullson stood scanning their surroundings. The sun found its way through cracks and beamed at their feet, a reflection caught their eyes; they stooped and observed a pendant — gold heart-shaped with the initial A.M inscribed on the underside. Mullson picked up the pendant and clenched it in his palm, his piercing eyes gazed the forest.

At an area where Bamboo trees towered above a stream and their leaves whistled in the cool morning breeze, Captain Austin approached a charred patch of land where the Black Stealth had earlier crashed. With a sniper rifle at hand and a duffel bag across his shoulder, he scanned every inch of the woods. When he thought the moment was right he tiptoed and snuck a peek into the plane, but nobody was aboard. Captain Austin whisked a two way radio to his mouth.

"Charlie one, over."

"Bravo one over," Mullson's voice crackled to life over the radio.

"This is Charlie one. Location, quadrant three, positive ID of missing Stealth Bomber."

"In Jamaica... you got to be kidding."

From the corner of an eye Captain Austin glanced and spotted a figure wearing a trench coat dodging behind some bamboo trees. A black coat he thought, as he tried to shuffle the image in his head, but the person had disappeared. Austin placed his left foot forward, slowly followed by the right, his intension was clear... to sneak his way behind the perpetrator and capture him, alive he hoped.

Captain Austin penetrated the bamboo field and spotted the mysterious figure in the black trench coat, standing facing away, just ahead. He pointed the rifle at the person's back; everything seemed to be under control as he looked through the scope and zeroed in on his target. He had no idea he now confronted one of the assassins who helped to annihilate his marines.

The assassin sensed Captain Austin, yet he did not show any sign of fear, even after glancing over his shoulder and seeing the rifle pointing in his direction. He stood and forced a boot against a bamboo lying in his path, which he snapped in half. The thought of surrendering did not come to mind. He chuckled. The old man turned out to be more resilient than he anticipated.

"Don't even think about it," Captain Austin warned.

"Next time I'll kill him for good," he promised, beneath his breath. He walked towards some of the thicker cluster of bamboos.

"Goodbye," Captain Austin whispered with a rush of confidence, after getting a feel for the wind. He took a deep breath and held it as he squeezed the trigger, gently. Right away he knew he had a kill as a bullet ripped through several bamboos and rocketed towards the back of the assassin's head, it's thunderous boom bounced off the top of nearby hills.

"Bravo one!" Detective Mullson's voice echoed from the CB radio Captain Austin had. "Do you read me?"

Captain Austin eyes were transfixed on his prey and he hadn't heard a word from the deafening CB. He wanted to pinch himself, for he knew the target was accurate and precise. As an expert rifleman he pretty much could pickoff a dime as far as the bullet would travel.

The assassin detected a whining sound that got louder and louder, his mind figured, but he waited for the boom to follow; and when it did he hurled his head to the left and only got his right ear blown off. He'd being beaten up for the past few days, but he rather not make that an excuse for slacking.

"Com'on," he encouraged himself, "These immortals are no match for me."

Captain Austin fired another round, again, again, and again — but the assassin eluded all three bullets. Austin clenched his fist and bit down on his cracked lip, he could taste the blood seeping into his mouth. He flipped two grenades.

While rotating in midair, the assassin pulled out two M10s from under his coat, and from each fired a bullet toward the grenades Austin had tossed at him. With a bullet hitting each of the grenades dead on, the force sent the grenades flying in the opposite direction, back toward Captain Austin who had already dove behind some bushes and tucked his head towards his chest.

Two abrupt explosions pierced the woods simultaneously to the blasting of a machine gun; birds took to the sky, rabbits and wild pigs scampered away, dogs matched their barks with the rumbling sounds bouncing off the top of hills. Detective Mullson and Jack heard the commotion and hurried towards the action. They fought their way through an area densely populated with thorns, till they reached a bamboo field. Johnny P shuffled towards Captain Austin who was covered by the aftermath of the grenades penetrating the ground. He fired at the assassin who dodged hundreds of bullets while gliding through the air and clinching to the top of the towering bamboos for support.

Most of the bamboo trees got mowed in a matter of seconds by the grazing bullets spitting out at the other end of Johnny P's overheated gun. All his life he'd convinced his friends he was a bad boy, the way he walked, talked, dressed, the perfect ingredients for masking the soft hearted person he was. With an assassin to kill, his heart slowly began to harden. The more the bastard continued to evade the reign of bullets, the more compelled Johnny became; his objective will not be denied. But things changed when the clicking sounds of the trigger echoed. He hurried as he began to lock in another chain of rounds.

From out of his duffle bag Captain Austin pulled out a miniature version of a M203 and pumped a grenade toward the assassin. The grenade separated into hundreds of shrapnel particles that rocketed forward. The assassin stared death in the eyes and knew his luck was running short. One of Engulf's soldiers emerged from behind the assassin.

The assassin darted behind the soldier for coverage and managed to survive the vicious encounter at the expense of his comrade. More soldiers from Engulf's Army closed in, but they were no match for Captain Austin.

The assassin huffed and puffed, he fired toward Johnny P and Captain Austin, this time his intent more deadly. No more playing around, although he did enjoy the old man's spirit. A true warrior indeed, but all good things must end.

From all the years of fighting for country, men, and God, the life of the captain had begun to dwindle, he'd done all he could, but the assassin finally outwitted him. During their short encounter he'd learned to respect the resilient man who he figured was enjoying the challenge a little too much. Some people kill for sport others for glory, but the assassin had a higher cause, as if the world was coming to an end and he will not be stopped.

Johnny P kneeled over Captain Austin whose life got snatched away by a bullet to the head, his soul departed before saying goodbye. He died proud with a smile across his face, looking as peaceful as ever. Johnny P was missing the old man who'd taught him so much in such a short time, a true friend that will be forever in his heart, like Murf and Pain Killer.

When his infuriating mind cleared he found no trace of the assassin lingering in the nearby woods. The snapping of twigs coming from behind had him pointing the machine gun in the direction.

Mullson stepped out into the clear. "Please put away the gun," he said, waiting for Johnny P to make a move. He tossed his bow and arrows into some nearby shrubs, in the direction of the river.

Johnny P eyed Mullson from head to toe. "You never like me anyway," he said, still pointing the gun. His finger pressed against the trigger, slowly.

"Don't!" Mullson bellowed, after he figured what was going on. With vengeance raging in his heart Johnny P squeezed the trigger; the roaring sounds overpowered Detective Mullson's voice that had being wailing in the background. When all the bullets were out and the smoke cleared Johnny P glanced at the man in the bloody Khaki suit, lying face down.

"What have I done?" he said.

"First time, isn't it?" said Mullson, after he got up from behind a patch of bush and brushed off his clothing. He walked over to the dead man who was wearing a similar khaki outfit. Minutes ticking away seemed like hours. A wide grin beamed across his face, he couldn't have asked for a better son in law, boy was he pleased. He came and stood next to Johnny P, then gave him a pat on the shoulder, gently. He stood back and glanced down at Captain Austin.

CHAPTER 17

As he Drifted further into the woods Engulf dragged Anna who'd being unconscious for the past few minutes by her hair; he came to a secluded area where he tossed aside branches used to conceal an oversized boulder. Behind the rock a tunnel appeared.

Anna wheezed when a whiff of urea hit her nose, when she opened her eyes she found herself in a cave with thousands of rats fighting to get out. She tried to scream, a few crackles at first, and finally the high pitch that woke the millions of bats clinging to the roof, they too followed the rats as they sought a way out.

"Where am I?" Anna wailed. "Where am I?" her voice echoed back.

As they continued to penetrate the cave inside it got darker and darker.

"How does it feel my dear Anna?" said Engulf.

"Stop touching me you freak!"

"What makes you think I'm touching you Miss Anna Mullson?"

"I want to go home!"

Engulf flicked on a lighter and lit a lantern hanging from the roof, revealing swarm of roaches, centipedes, spiders, decades of human remains, mounds of bat droppings.

Anna screamed her soul out, she'd realized her captor was not molesting her; instead creepy crawlers were to be blame for the tickling sensation moving up her legs. She was no longer constrained by Engulf's mighty hands. She gathered her strength and spun around, with the intent to set herself free, and almost collide with a human creature — the person stood tall in her path, streaks of linen bound the body from neck to toes, the head unwrapped, exposing a mummified skull. With arms extended the creature toddled forward.

Anna froze in her track, her head pounded, goose bumps rose on her arms and legs, a sudden chill hit her face as a gust of wind came out of nowhere.

The last gleam of sunlight that had being beaming from the horizon disappeared beyond the Caribbean Sea. Sporadic winds ripped across the water, yet the waves were calm like most Sundays. In the distance a small church stood at the foot of a hill; Detective Mullson and Johnny P hurried toward it. The night got blackened as the minutes past. Closer to the church the sounds made by the wind got louder, as if cats were among the bushes crying like babies.

Johnny P listened to the wailing wind and had a sense of guilt plaguing his conscience, a burning sensation piercing his heart worsened.

Mullson opened the gate and entered the churchyard; Johnny P tailed him.

Inside the church Father Johnson had been kneeling, before darkness had descended and the raging storm threatened.

"Blessed be the lord my rock," he said, "Who trains my hands for war and my fingers for battle."

With night approaching they shifted towards the center of the church — Father Johnson, Magarette Mullson and her mother sat praying.

Pastor James, the local Minster, went and locked every window and door. He was about late forties, still sporting his favorite Sunday suit that he'd worn earlier — grey pants and jacket with a matching tie, and a white shirt underneath. He swatted away sweat collected on his forehead, for outside the pungent scent of the Noni fruit had been following the wind, to him this represented evil as indicated by the local Jamaican myth: when spirits were near the stronger the aroma.

A bang against the door had Pastor James scurrying.

The Sunday night service had been canceled, complaints of ghostly activities in the neighborhood made some of the people scared out of their wits, nobody was supposed to be heading this side, Pastor James hesitated.

"Who goes there?" he said, his bass voice whispered from the other side.

"It's me Pastor James," said Mullson, hoping the man would recognize his voice. After a few seconds the door was ajar. Johnny P nodded discreetly to the man who was standing by the door.

A sigh of relief beamed across Pastor James' face. "Welcome home gentlemen," he said.

Johnny P moved ahead of Detective Mullson.

"Thank you," he said, slightly bracing against the door.

Before entering Mullson glanced over his shoulder and spotted someone staring at him with glowing eyes, further from the church, he couldn't see the face. A second look and the figure was gone, what's happening, his mind raced, but he tried not to show any sign of fear.

Mullson and Johnny P headed towards the center of the church. Pastor James turned the key then slid a bolt to secure the door.

"Man will fall," he said, walking behind the two. "But will rise again to fight another day."

"Thanks for the encouragement Pastor James," said Mullson.

"Where is my baby?" said Mrs. Mullson. She shuffled to her feet and tossed herself into the strong grip of her husband's arms. "Please find her!" she pleaded with tears running down her cheeks. She eventually calmed and stood back.

Mullson glanced down for the sixth or seventh time at his wife's necklace and observed the pendant, resembling the one he had found earlier. "I will find her," he promised, his intense eyes surveyed the room.

Mrs. Mullson's mother went and stood by her family; she gave them a big hug. "Everything goanna be alright," she said.

Johnny P went and gave Mrs. Mullson a hug. "How're you my son?" she asked.

"I'm alright Mrs. Mullson," he replied. "We'll find Anna… even if we have to search every inch of this country."

They all went and joined Father Johnson who was on the floor meditating the whole time. Facing the inside they sat in a circle holding hands. "Blessed is the man who walks not in the counsel of the ungodly." said Pastor James, with eyes closed.

A few hours had passed. The human circle remained sturdy. "I have to!" Detective Mullson bellowed, after a brief discussion. He finally broke the link.

"Not yet my son," Father Johnson warned him.

"Please don't," Magarette pleaded to her husband. "At least wait until tomorrow."

"Just say yuh attempts," said Pastor James, to Mull-son. "How on earth would yuh survive? First yuh have to battle the elements, then the darkness. Either is enough to drive a man crazy. Let's get prepared." He hurried to a room located at the back of the church, beyond the pulpit, where he retrieved a few items like: holy water, crosses, and flashlights — all these to aid in the fight against evil.

In the backdrop the squawking of crows filled the air. For the past forty years Pastor James had never heard anything of this sort taking place here, well, maybe not entirely true. He recalled an incident when he was about eight years old: crows had descended over where the old hospital once stood, not too far away, where a massacre took place. That had been the only time the crow came at night, and this time he hoped no one suffered the same faith.

He jogged towards a window and peeped through a crack. There was something out there that had the hair at the back of his neck rise, and his knees wobbled from the weight of his upper body. Pastor James rubbed his eyes, a man was standing at the outskirts of his church, he could have sworn. A distinct glow from the creature's eyes that stood out in his mind, as they stared at him from beyond a cowl tossed over the head, it reminded him of his black cat whenever she crouches outside at night.

Mullson went and stood beside Pastor James who seemed a little disturbed. He peeped through the window;

at the outer limits stood the mysterious figure he thought he'd spotted earlier. The creature gazed longingly into his eyes. Mullson did the same and overpowered the darkness — the blood he cried had cleansed the creature of its curse. For the past forty years the woman under the cowl had being searching for her two baby boys that had being whisked away from her. Her soul finally found peace as the light burst from her body and rocketed into heaven. The squawking of crows also ended.

The guilt of losing his mother at birth got lifted from his heart, somehow Mullson sensed his spirit was connected to the lady and he whispered, "Goodbye."

Closer to where the Black Stealth had crashed, soldiers from Engulf's army prowled in the darkest of night. Six of them came and evaluated the plane. The sudden chirping of birds got their attention, a long silence followed, but they were vigilant.

The night came alive as bullets riddled the bodies of Engulf's militia. Jamaican soldiers, dressed for guerrilla warfare, emerged from the landscape. Two soldiers took it upon themselves to put several bullets into the heads of Engulf's falling soldiers.

"Now yu dead fi real," one of them said. A clapping sound reverberated but nobody could pinpoint the origin.

"Good job," a voice said, coming from all angles of the woods, as if megaphones were planted on every tree.

The sky suddenly became blackened and the night dreaded.

"Who that?" soldiers hollered. "Yu playing with fire!"

The eerie voice had them shuffling in an outward ring formation; like the effects of fallen dominoes their fingers hit the triggers and the darkness got colored red by tracers. A sudden silence followed. The soldiers waited, meanwhile contemplating their next move. They grew tough and despised cowardice, no human was able to break them, and now for the first time they felt fear cuddling their hearts, something was still lurking out there — they sensed it.

"I am Engulf," the voice taunted, "Son of Satan. But today I am God!"

Engulf appeared out of thin air and began to move back and forth, at superhuman speed, his intention deadly.

The soldiers fired with conviction. That didn't deter the killing machine.

The piercing sounds of human terror and gunshots were drowned out by raging wind and excessive thunder that devoured the land, suddenly. Lightning illuminated the forest where Engulf stood, around him piled carcasses of mutilated bodies, as if attacked by wild beasts.

CHAPTER 18

The wind had kicked up a few knots ripping apart trees and sending sheets of zinc from roofs located miles away cutting through the air. Vivid streaks of lights across the sky followed by thunderous booms that had being shaking the earth, intensified. Like a giant photoflash the lights brightened the forest where Assassin #1 roamed near an overflowing river shoving boulders, vehicles, and other debris towards the sea. Detective Mullson, Jack, and Johnny P, hidden beneath their ponchos, used their headlamp flashlights and battled their way through the dark, until they reached a part of the forest drenched with blood diluted by the pouring rain, where fallen soldiers from the Jamaican Defense Force and Engulf's army scattered.

Nothing around Jack goes unnoticed, not even the pouring rain could drown the reek of blood and marijuana he sniffed out, a task considered challenging for a bloodhound, he looked at the ground as he came to a crawl. "We have company," he whispered.

Mullson gripped the M16 tighter and scanned the area. Johnny P wanted to fire a few warning shots. "This place gives me the creeps!" he admitted.

"Run!" Mullson screamed. Detective Mullson and Johnny tumbled and ducked as they scrambled away.

Soldiers from the JDF who'd buried themselves in the mud sprouted. They'd been waiting to avenge their comrades who'd given their lives to protect a country in a war yet to be declared.

Mullson glanced over his shoulder and didn't see Jack; to him it wasn't a major concern since Jack always managed to elude the enemies. He'd been more than unconventional, but Mullson left him alone, as always. Anna was his focus and if Jack can help, let it be. The man hated church, only showed interest in holidays like Halloween and Columbus Day, but to Mullson he'd been a good partner.

The soldiers fired a few rounds as they closed in on two intruders zigzagging ahead.

"Lights out!" said Mullson, to Johnny P, after realizing they couldn't shake the men tailing them. They switched off their headlamps and dove behind some bushes where they laid.

With a flashlight in one hand a soldier came and stopped next to them, he moved the beams closer to Detective Mullson who spotted the light and positioned his gun to shoot.

"Retrieve!" a man shouted.

They pulled away.

Mullson heaved a sigh of relief.

Dawn approached. Inside the church lit by candles held high in iron scones, Pastor James, Mrs. Mullson and her mom were on the floor sleeping. Father Johnson had been awake the entire night observing a knife keenly; the one he believed belongs to Satan.

"At the crow of dawn," he said. "Prepare to fight. God be with you my children." The loud shrill cry of roosters erupting in the backdrop rejuvenated the start of morning, followed by the barking of dogs, the twittering of birds, and the rumbling of motor engines.

Mullson had not travelled as far as he initially planned. To be exact, six hours had passed since him and Johnny P had been hiding behind some branches chopped and tossed aside; they were eager to get back on track to go search for Anna.

Mullson took a whiff. "What's that smell?" he said.

Johnny P took a deep breath; his stomach turned by a familiar stench blowing about. "What's wrong with ya friend?" he said.

"My friend?"

"Jack… is he afraid of the church?"

"That you have to ask him."

"He's an ungodly nigga," said Johnny, he seemed somewhat uncomfortable as Mullson glanced towards him. "Sorry. Where's the knife?"

Mullson hesitated. "It's safe," he finally said. "That's all you need to know." His eyes swept the forest floor. "Did you hear that?"

"What?" said Johnny P, pulling an ear as he zoomed in on the crowing of roosters and the growling of dogs bouncing off the distant hills, and around him, the chirping of birds and the sounds of rushing water, neither of which the detective was referring to.

Mullson darted to his feet and begun to search among the branches littering the ground, until he accidentally stumbled upon a cave.

Inside, it took a moment for their eyes to get accustomed to their surroundings. The lights radiating from their flashlights brightened the place, revealing bat droppings, human remains, rodents, and other creepy crawlers. With their bodies tingling uncomfortably Mullson and Johnny held their noses and advanced slowly, further in, the confinement appeared smaller. They spotted a mummified body resting in one corner. Mullson, while gripping his gun and moving closer to the body, signaled the youngster to go stand guard at the entrance. Johnny P who'd already swung around stopped and listened. He doubled back to where Mullson stood staring at the light bouncing off the back wall, revealing a horde of insects. With jaws dropped the two began to retreat when the buzzing got more threatening by the seconds.

They sprinted towards the exit. The insects launched an aerial and ground attack. With flying insects nearing their backs they dropped their weapons and pumped their arms faster, a river popped up ahead, they closed in.

The flooded waters had receded, but, nevertheless it continued to shove boulders and other large objects in the direction heading to sea. Upstream was less muddy, where Engulf glided through the water and crossed to the other side. Assassin #1 followed his leader; the powerful river was no match for their cunningness. The assassin dragged Anna by her legs that had been bound with duck tape. On the bank, she laid with water pouring from her mouth and ears, she coughed. Anna struggled to set herself free, her effort proven futile. Blood began to seep from the bottom of her feet, from spots where prickles jutted out.

"Your father interrupted the mission," Assassin #1 reminded Engulf.

"What is he doing here?" said Engulf, sounding dis-appointed.

Downstream, Mullson and Johnny jumped into the river as the insects clung to them, but other dangers rushed along. The current dragged them under and spit them up, twisted and twirled; they struggled to set free. At one bank a fallen tree protruding above the water was within Mullson's grasp, and he got a break, in time to stretch a hand and pulled Johnny P till he got a hold of a branch. After gathering enough energy they heaved their carcasses out of the water, on the bank where they sprawled out and gazed at the sun. It was still early in the morning, but no time for resting.

Jack had been missing since last night and Mullson now began to get anxious. The guilt of what happened to Captain Austin ripped his heart apart, his missing daughter, oh God… please protect her from all evil. Should he contact the police or continue searching? He sensed more danger ahead and wished he didn't lose his weapons; the thought quickly dwindled from his head when he realized he'll have to cross the river to fetch them. A smile beamed on his face as he began to survey the area, until he spotted his bow and arrows beneath some dried leaves. Good thinking paid off, Mullson credited himself. Yesterday before the river flooded its banks he crossed over and tossed them there, all right. Johnny P was pointing a machine gun at him. Destiny is a funny thing Mullson admitted.

Along the bank of the river Johnny P and Detective Mullson headed upstream, following three sets of footprints plastered in the mud — two pairs of boots and a barefoot with a trace of blood. The river winded vigorously through the valley. They were on the right trail, but they had no idea. Mullson got excited and raced ahead. Further up the path the foot prints had disappeared, but they continued to follow tiny pieces of clothing placed at random as if to mark the trail.

Assassin #1 stood eying the man who'd been tailing their tracks. He knew everything about Mullson: his secrets, passions, the selfless love for his family. The last time they met he got embarrassed by a wardrobe malfunction. Behind, Engulf left the assassin to do his dirty bidding, he could have easily snap a finger and get the work done himself, but with the Mullsons twin, things were a bit more complicated. As powerful as Engulf was he feared the prophecy, but would not admit.

Mullson stopped after spotting a man who seemed threatening and fitted an arrow in his bow then aimed to the side. Johnny P finally came tumbling into Mullson who'd come to a standstill. They shuffled towards the man.

"That's him," said Johnny P, pointing towards the assassin.

"I know," whispered Mullson, not fully comprehending.

"You're a real nice guy," said Johnny P. "If that was my house he burnt down, I would smoke him like a piece of bacon. I'm still goanna smoke that mother-fucker for killing ma boys."

Detective Mullson's eyes focused on the assassin, anger raged through his body, he'd just realized what Johnny P was referring to.

"My mother fucking house?" he said.

"Yes your mother excuse me house," Johnny P repeated, "You better whop his ass."

Further up trail Engulf had just darted around a bend; Anna who'd being under his spell followed like a zombie. Her hands and feet were no longer bound. In her head she heard voices of her father and her boyfriend Johnny, but couldn't respond.

Engulf came to an open area, off in the distance luscious green hills seemed to touch heaven, and most notable were the excessive numbers of butterflies fluttering across the plain.

"Tell daddy goodbye you sweet little thing," Engulf told her. His words were followed by darkness devouring the day that became night.

Mullson wondered what was happening as he stared at the sky. Johnny P must have been thinking the same thing too, but there was no time to figure, the assassin came charging toward them. Mullson pointed his arrow, a little too late, a fist connected his midriff sent him sprawling. Johnny P became dazed after a kick to the head jerked his brain. The assassin kicked and punched, Mullson and

Johnny P kept getting up, over and over. The assassin pointed a small gun at Detective Mullson and fired.

In a flash Johnny P dove before Detective Mullson when he spotted the gun.

CHAPTER 19

At a section of the woodland dominated by ciders and oaks, Jack confronted a man hidden among the shadows. A ray of light glistened through the trees as the sun passed above, the cool morning breeze faded, birds stop chirping, no more dogs growling, as if nature took a break.

"You seem to forget who we are," said Agent Hill, his fierce eyes scanned Jack's every move.

"I'm still in command!" Jack bellowed.

Agent Hill chuckled. "Not anymore," he teased. "Why don't you cut me in on the deal and I might reconsider," more evil chuckles.

"Remember your girlfriend."

"You killed Agent McKoy, didn't you?"

"What difference does it make?" said Agent Hill. He began to laugh out of control. "She will still find time for you in hell."

"You just got the devil crossed," Jack whispered. "Bad move mister-"

Agent Hill punched Jack, launching him through the air, before he got a chance to break his fall he hurled him in another direction. Jack bounced off a tree and hit the ground with a thud. He got up and they fought, with incredible strength and speed, the forest trembled beneath their feet.

Jack disappeared.

An object the size of a bullet penetrated Agent Hill and ricocheted off his ribs, crushing them, the flesh beneath his skin began to eat away. Only two people in the universe could have done what had been happening to him, God and —

The day had turned into night as predicted. The knife Engulf lost and had been seeking must be driven into the heart of his father for Engulf to become the leader of the fire world. Agent Hill was promised second in command, but all his power got consumed by someone more powerful than he'd imagined, and he realized that bastard was tricking them all along. His mind raged with furry, how could this happen?

"Impossible!" he yelled, before his lifeless body hit the ground—

Within the carcass something moved from the chest to the bowel, as if alive. The skin busted open and an angel with horns towering above his head emerged and stood tall.

"Jack is back," his voiced thundered. He was given a second chance to reign over his kingdom, for that he was grateful, and the twisted sacrifice by mankind showed him how unpredictable human nature can be. He clinched his fists and looked to the sky, anxiously awaited to exert his presence, but first he must warn the others, at the dark sky he pointed and day returned.

Earlier darkness clouded the morning sky, Father Johnson, Pastor James, Mrs. Mullson and her mother were all worried. Inside the church they sat waiting. Father Johnson begged the lord for more time, he knew what must be done to level the playing field; three years ago Father Andrew let him in on a secret, one which haunted Father Johnson ever since.

Father Johnson ran his fingers along the edge of a knife, the one Engulf lost in Anna's room, Satan's knife. He sensed the end was near, the warm blood rushing through his veins doubled as he raised the knife to his chest, all he thought about — picrcing his heart with this particular knife will set evil free. Well, only a myth for now.

Everybody had panic written all over their faces when they spotted Father Johnson raise the knife to his chest. "Please don't!" Mrs. Mullson pled.

"There is no other choice," said Father Johnson, his mind already made up. "I have to join Father Andrew."

"Setting the devil free is not an option!" Pastor James yelled at Father Johnson, he'd read a passage from the book 'Secrets to Life.'

"The prophecy must be fulfilled," said Father Johnson, before driving the knife into his own heart.

Johnny P had a burning sensation rushing from his chest to his abdomen that intensified by the seconds, a blurry vision had him staggering. On the ground, in a puddle of blood he rolled and groaned, till he passed out.

Detective Mullson stooped over and pressed his palms against Johnny's midriff, in the meantime glimpsing at the assassin from the corner of an eye. The gushing blood began to subside.

"Stay awake!" said Mullson, slapping Johnny P's face, over and over.

The assassin stared at them, one down one to go. Mullson grabbed his bow; the assassin fired at Mullson and hit him square in the right arm causing him to drop the bow.

Detective Mullson bit down on his teeth, an excruciating pain made him paralyzed, but he fought and set himself free. With another attempt he fit a special arrow with razor sharp teeth aligning the length of the body in the bow; while running towards the assassin he aimed with deadly intent.

Having done many tricks in circuses before, the assassin braced himself as the arrow rocketed toward him, this should be easy, he thought. As the arrow neared his chest he got a grip, real firm, only this time something went strangely wrong — several of his fingers went flying, his chest and back ripped opened. He came towards Mullson.

They continued to fight till they were breathless. Mullson, with a burst of extraordinary strength, destroyed his opponent.

Peace at last for the soul of the assassin who'd being roaming the earth for the past thousand years, he realized Mullson was the chosen one to rid the earth of fallen angels, one of the few humans who possesses the gift to change the universe, the last hope for mankind, if they believe...   As the assassin's life wiggled away he stretched his hand to give Mullson an envelope he'd been hiding in an inside pocket of his trench coat.

"Save yourself," he whispered.

Thinking he was trying to pull a quick one, Detective Mullson ignored the envelope. In his head a glimpse of his enemy flashed — a ninja assassin who jumped from a sixth floor window and lived to fight another day. But, why was the stranger after him and his family?

The man died with an outreached arm.

Detective Mullson flicked away the envelope and tore it open; inside he found a picture of Nina and himself entering a hotel room. All along somebody had been stalking him, yet he had no clue. He dropped the envelope, tiny pieces of cloth, resembling those on the trail, scattered on the ground. He shredded the picture to pieces.

"Thank you whoever you are," he said, looking down at the man he just killed.

Johnny P stirred for the first time since being unconscious. "Go get Anna," he said, to Mullson. "I will be okay."

Without hesitating, Mullson scurried ahead, totally forgetting his bow and arrow. He wound around a bend and spotted Engulf shoving Anna to the ground. Mullson's heart raced, he ground his teeth, but tried to show no sign of anger.

"Why are you doing this to us?" he asked as he edged towards Engulf. "I don't even know you."

Engulf eyed Mullson coldly. "Does the name Engulf ring a bell?" he said, followed by an evil laugh that had goose bumps popping up at the back of Mullson's neck. "Where is my knife?"

"What knife?" Mullson replied.

Engulf extended his arms, palms up, and rose them toward the sky; Anna's enervated body hoisted simultaneously to him raising his arms, she laid high above the ground as if held by some sort of invisible force. "Now that I've got your attention-" Engulf threatened Mullson.

"Please don't," Detective Mullson pleaded while gaping at his daughter, "I'm telling the truth. I don't know what you're talking about!"

Engulf dropped his hand to his side. Anna plummeted to the ground where she laid unconscious.

Detective Mullson rushed to her aid, but got tossed in the opposite direction by Engulf's supernatural power, and hit his head against a tree. When he jumped to his feet the place spun like he'd just exited a merry-go-round, blurry images of his enemy stood watching. Mullson touched a spot on his head, painful at first, where blood spurted from a wound.

Humans were considered inferior to his kind, but this Mullson man Engulf admired for his perseverance, maybe he got lucky against the assassin, the thought had crossed his mind.

Mullson sprinted toward Engulf and fought with all his might, but the invincible Engulf dominated, effortlessly.

"I'm going to teach you how to become a man," Engulf jeered, "Just the way I taught your brother."

A battered Mullson tried to control the anger raging inside him; glancing over his shoulder he spotted his daughter lying still, tears trickled down his cheeks. Clenching his jaws and fists he moved closer to Engulf.

"The time has come," Mullson whispered.

"I will not quit until I rule heaven and earth!" Engulf bellowed.

"That which was united will now be broken."

Engulf chuckled an evil laugh. "The prophecy," he blurted. "Fairy tales have no place in my world."

Blood trickled from Mullson's eyes.

"Look into my eyes," he said; all along he thought he was oozing tears.

Engulf staggered.

"Impossible!" he said.

Mullson used his hands and wiped away what he initial thought were tears.

"His power is useless," he whispered to himself, after he saw a confused Engulf backing away, yet he didn't figure what was slowing him.

A horrendous pain ran through Engulf's body whenever Mullson punched him. A pair of wings shredded his upper clothing as they emerged from his back.

"Keep that blood away from me!" a terrified Engulf pleaded.

Mullson grabbed one of Engulf's wings and pulled with all his might till he ripped it from his back; he did the same to the remaining wing.   Engulf pierced the air with a high-pitched cry, demons departed his body; souls of those who he'd conquered were free at last.

"How does it feel to be disloyal?" Jack's voice echoed from the woods.

"Help me father!" screamed Engulf.

"Couldn't have said it better," said the voice, amongst the shadows.

The devil came swiftly toward Engulf and whisked him away, they disappeared.

Detective Mullson stood transfixed. "This can't be," he said. He went and stooped by his daughter who was still unconscious.

Jason, with his head reattached, appeared out of thin air and stood tall. His wing span extended more than fifteen feet. Mullson hoped this man came in peace. Jason moved closer.

"You have the power to do whatever you wish," he said, extending an arm, "But only once will it be granted."

A smile beamed across Mullson's face as he shook Jason's hand. The stranger tapped Anna on her forehead before vanishing. Anna jumped to her feet and wondered where the three little boys went. She had no recollection of Engulf, the roaring river, Annic Palmer or the bloody water. In Anna's mind, she was still enjoying the peaceful Sunday evening, but it felt weird, as if it was morning. Her clothes were raggedy, her flip-flops nowhere to be found.

"Dad," she said, when she spotted her father. "What are you doing here?"

He gave her a big hug. "Long story," he replied.

CHAPTER 20

I n Montego Bay evening had approached. Mullson, with Johnny P braced against his chest, rushed toward Pastor James's church. Anna followed closely. When Mullson got to the church he placed Johnny P on a patch of grass. Pastor James spotted them and came to assist. Johnny P's condition worsened; whenever he became unconscious it was for a much longer period.

Mrs. Mullson's face beamed with excitement as she ran toward Anna; she hugged her daughter, joyful tears flooded her cheeks. "I will never leave you again," she said, "I promise."

Anna was glad to see her mother. "I'm okay mom," she said, rushing to get back to Johnny P.

"Are you sure my child?" asked her grandmother.

"I will be okay grandma," said Anna. After giving her grandmother a hug she came and stood by Johnny P. "Why are they taking so long?" she continued, sounding hysterical.

Johnny P began to quiver out of control, as if undergoing shock.

"Everything's gonna be alright my son," said Magarette.

"Please don't leave me," Anna wept, "I love you boo…"

A pickup roared in the backdrop, out yonder Detective Mullson spotted it heading his direction.

"Where is the blasted ambulance?" he said…

Along a windy and narrow country road, an old Chevy four by four pickup raced toward the town. Hills painted green with vegetation dominated the backdrop, at both side of the road trees towered, flowers and ferns flourished, straight ahead, at the bottom of a hill, the sea seemed to touch the sky. A few children, barefoot, scurried along a path leading from the road to a river below; the thundering horn of the pick had a handcart driver tucked away in a patch of bush, near a bend.

At the back of the truck, Detective Mullson and Pastor James sat tending to Johnny P who'd been crouching on the floor.

Anna, Mrs. Mullson and her mom were stuffed inside the truck next to Mr. Busy.

"Oh my God!" said Anna.

Mr. Busy swung the truck right, barely missing a dog standing in the road.

"I am a very successful businessman," he bragged. At the main road he made a right turn in the left lane. "I man control the bus service, the car service… even the ambulance service."

Anna chewed away at her finger nails.

Mrs. Mullson, who was in no mood for chitchat, glanced at the odometer approaching eighty-five kilometer per hour. "Step on it you punk!" she said, to Mr. Busy.

The truck gave a sudden burst of energy as it sped through the town, made a sharp right, and ahead approached the hospital. Mullson and Pastor James battled the wind to prevent falling from the back of the truck.

The truck swung around and backed up to the front entrance of the hospital. A sudden downpour sent them dashing towards the entrance, a nurse signaled a porter to wheel the patient to the operating room.

Inside the hospital, for the past three hours, Detective Mullson and his family had been waiting in the crowded lobby. They sat on chairs shoved against the wall. Anna shook out of control, she hugged her grandmother.

Magarette rested her head against her husband's chest and listened to his heartbeat. "Your mom would be proud of you," she said, rubbing a hand against his rock-hard chest.

"If they hadn't murdered her," he blurted.

Mrs. Mullson's jaws dropped. "Thought she died in labor?"

"That's what I thought… let's not talk about it."

"Where is Jack?"

Mullson looked serious for a moment, his heart pounded faster, sweat splattered over his forehead, his fingers began to twitch out of control — he was quite certain Jack was alive. His voice echoed from the woods, but the figure that came and snatched away Engulf had horns jutting from the forehead like a Texas Long Horn Bull, blazing eyes, and wings extending more than fifteen feet across. Mullson recalled how he couldn't move for fear.

"He went home," he whispered.

Magarette figured her husband had enough and thought best to leave him alone, he might not say much, but he's a good man who protected his family at all costs.

Captain Austin and Jack had come and gave their all, a grateful Mullson will always remember them, true friends indeed.

It was late into the night when two doctors entered the lobby and came toward the Mullson family who had being struggling to stay awake— with the exception of Anna. She sensed they came with updates regarding Johnny P.

Anna got up and moved swiftly toward a woman and a man. "Is he okay," she said, "Please tell me he's alright."

"We are sorry," the man said. "We tried out best."

"It was a little too late," the woman added.

The whole family had come and stood listening. Anna hugged her mom, they cried.

Detective Mullson looked the woman in the eyes. "Doc," he said. "Can I take a look?"

"Sure," the woman agreed, glancing at her partner.

They hurried along a hallway until they reached a side door where they entered a small room.

Inside, Mullson stared at Johnny P's lifeless body, partially covered and resting on a table. "Give me a few minutes by myself," he said.

The female doctor signaled her colleagues to leave the room.

Mullson had one choice, the temptation overbearing, of all the possibilities he'd lingering in his brain — happiness and financial security should have ranked the highest among his priorities. God, only if he'd more than one wish, how about wishing for more wishes? Not gonna work, only one to be granted. Mullson had been leaning towards Jason's promise; with his mind already made up he blurted the words and waited.

Early the following morning Detective Mullson and his family were dressed; on Mrs. Mullson mother's porch they stood waiting for their taxi to take them to the airport.

Further along a rocky road, Pastor James strode towards the house; he shoved aside the metal gate and entered the front yard. "Good morning everybody," he greeted.

"Good morning Pastor James," they said.

He climbed to the patio and entered the front door leading to the living room; Mr. Mullson and Anna followed him.

Inside the living room several suitcases were stacked neatly on the floor, a what-not shoved to one side of the room had a television playing.

Pastor James came and stood before Detective Mullson.

"Have a nice trip," he said. "We surely going to miss yuh guys." He handed Mullson an old book. "Father Johnson left it for yuh," he continued.

Mullson took the book and observed the cover, the name read: Secrets to life. "Thank you," he said, after securing the book under his arm.

The rumbling of a car sent Anna dashing towards the patio. "Dad," she called. "The taxi is here."

"Lets go Kevin!" said Detective Mullson, moving toward the front exit.

From the dining room Johnny P entered the living room and came to the front door. "It's all the same," he said. "Johnny P, Kevin, what's ma name."

It was ten o'clock on a gloomy morning in New York and Detective Mullson was making a quick stop at the first of two cemeteries he'd planned to visit. Although about an hour from the city, it took him almost two hours to reach his destination. He limped over the grass, all the way to a podium at one corner of the field where a FBI agent stood talking to his colleagues.

"Agent McKoy and Agent Hill were both wonderful people," he said. "We'll not stop searching until we find his body. As for Miss McKoy, may her soul rest in peace."After the ceremony concluded Mullson jumped in his Porsche and sped away, by the time he got back to the city evening had come.

At the second cemetery Detective Mullson stood by a grave and wept. In the distance a mysterious gentleman approached. The man was about Mullson's height and build, well dressed, carrying a shopping bag.

Mullson for what must have been the millionth time scanned the headstone.

✝

Father Eugene Andrew
1953 - 2018

Got to be a mistake, his mind kept wondering, the year 2020 has not yet ended, and Father Andrew was alive a week ago, wasn't he?

The mysterious gentleman came and stood behind him. "I'm sorry," his squeaky voice echoed. He placed the bag on the ground. "This is yours, a gift from—"

Mullson was so caught up in the year Father Andrew died he didn't realize someone stood behind him.

It was two years ago to be exact that Father Andrew had committed the unthinkable; at least that's what many people thought after months of speculation. The church had banished his name; to them his crime far worse than a murder. Only Father Andrew knew what had happened. On numerous occasions he gave his version of the story, but people kept ignoring him as if his words meant nothing. He knew he had to tell Mullson the truth.

He recalled holding a metal cross above his head that attracted a bolt of lightning, he was shaking out of control then a spirit leaped out of his body and hovered in midair. The figure watched him as he chanted, "The work of God is stronger than evil!" As the cross fell from his hands and hit the roof, he found himself disappearing into a cloud of fog. He now realized he got tricked by the spirit. Father Andrew had cast himself out of his body, as he fell toward the street below his faded voice echoed, "Help…"

"You have done all you could," Detective Mullson whispered at the grave. "It's okay to let go."

Mullson turned around after he felt the presence of somebody behind him, but the man had exited the cemetery. The fellow ripped off a facial mask, revealing his true identity as Wrath.

Again Mullson stared at the headstone and couldn't grasp the idea of Father Andrew being a ghost who died two years earlier before he met him. The creepy thought made him jump to his feet, bouncing over the shopping bag from which the head of a teenage boy rolled out. The boy who got abducted in the Bronx while purchasing ice cream, the one Mullson blamed himself for failing to protect.

About the Author

"I noticed you leave your daughter in the car," said R.J.

"It's a boy," a lady blurted then faced away.

Doing the right thing is never a good idea, especially in the world R.J. Green created filled with chaos, uncertainty, family morals, Gods, hatred, fantasy — a reality where people fell in love with Tanny Anderson, Detective Mullson, Jack, and are captivated by Engulf's power and Wrath's curse. A writer with an imagination larger than life, who's not afraid to provoke, intrigue...

R.J. Green is currently living in Florida, has a daughter, and is the owner of Masta Recka Publishing Co. BMI.